BAD
ELEMENTS

BAD
ELEMENTS

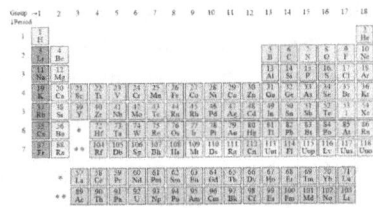

GARY ALEXANDER

**The New
Atlantian Library**

The New Atlantian Library

is an imprint of

ABSOLUTELY AMAZING eBOOKS

Published by Whiz Bang LLC, 926 Truman Avenue, Key West, Florida 33040, USA.

For information contact:
Publisher@AbsolutelyAmazingEbooks.com

ISBN-13: 978-1945772023 (The New Atlantian Library)
ISBN-10: 1945772026

BAD
ELEMENTS

There are 118 known elements on and in this planet. For whatever reason, a goodly number of them end in *-ium,* including 10 in this fable.

The largest-numbered elements, like the tongue-twisting ununseptium (117) and ununoctium (118) were corralled in a laboratory. Some have a half-life of from here to the end of this sentence. By the time you've finished reading this yarn, some may even have a use.

We'll be dealing with 34 of the more practical elements. Some are sexy, like gold. Some are dangerous, arsenic prominent among them.

Hopefully, none will be boring.

1.

ALUMINUM. *A soft, silvery, ductile metal with the symbol Al; Atomic number 13; Specific gravity 2.7.*

The stuff is everywhere. It's the third most abundant element on the planet after oxygen and silicon. However, aluminum seldom occurs in natural form. Instead, it's found combined with 270 different minerals.

Until the 1800s, nobody knew how to extract the metal from the ore. The first pure metal verged on priceless. Napoleon served his most important guests on aluminum plates. Middling nobility had to settle for gold and silver.

Nowadays, much aluminum is throwaway, megatons in the form of foil. A few ultra-pricey cars have aluminum bodies and are not throwaway. Nor are airplanes, which couldn't get off the ground if not made of aluminum.

Aluminum is attractive and decorative too. In Quito, Ecuador, there is a statue of a Madonna atop a hill. It's 150 feet tall and made of 7000 pieces of aluminum.

Much aluminum, primarily beverage cans, is recycled. The average lifespan of an aluminum beverage can is six weeks, from the time it's made, filled, sold, consumed, recycled and remanufactured, the same as an adult butterfly.

To date, close to a trillion beverage cans have been recycled.

Chuck's Waste Management and Recycling was one such concern. Chuck's was the largest recycling outfit in three counties. Though not apparent in any paperwork, Chuck's was owned by the Ripugnante crime family, which owned Chuck as well.

So when Chuck's Waste Management and Recycling's Chuck discovered a body inside a mountain of aluminum cans, he notified his superiors. Antonio (Tony Whack Job) Spazento was dispatched to see what the fuss was all about.

"What? Where?" Tony said before he slammed the Cadillac's door shut.

"The a-a-a-aluminum," Chuck said, a finger quivering toward it. "Thisaway."

"You said a body when you called the number. You should not have said 'body'. The b-word is a no-no. The airwaves have ears."

Chuck scratched deeply inside his coveralls and said, "Sorry. I know. I was rattled."

Chuck wasn't as rattled then as he was now in the presence of Tony Whack Job. He knew that the moniker was a double entendre, even though he didn't know what "double entendre" meant. Tony whacked people out for the Ripugnantes and he was, well, a little funny in the head, a little wacky.

Actually it was a triple entendre, if there was such a thing. Tony drove his victims to remote locations, whacked them into pieces, and buried them hither and yon. Occasionally, random body parts that were discovered. By then, though, they were harder to identify than The Unknown Soldier.

"Where?"

"Over there on the back side."

"Who else knows?"

"Only Dick, my kid brother. He was working the forklift. After he went and puked his guts out, he promised not to say nothing."

Tony smiled and slapped Chuck on the back. "You did well. Lead the way, bucko."

Antonio Spazento had a glorious white-toothed smile and perfect hair. He dressed out of a fashion magazine and wore just so much cologne. A gold Rolex and a tastefully-subdued sapphire pinky ring completed the ensemble. That Tony Whack Job looked and spoke like a TV anchorman terrified Chuck even more.

Chuck did lead the way, taking Spazento past the adjoining Chuck's Classic Car Pasture. The cream of that crop was a doorless 1977 Buick Electra 225 up on blocks.

They hopped aboard a forklift and rode up to a rise. Gesturing downward, Chuck said, "My cars I keep over yonder. We went by them in case you didn't notice. Junked out cars that get flattened, they're there. Them and other scrap tin. The gross shit and garbage I — "

"Fascinating, but you can conduct the guided tour some other time, yes?"

"Yes sir. Sorry."

On the opposite side of the aluminum cans, below a spongy mound emitting dangerous levels of methane gas, Chuck stopped and pointed down at the aforementioned body, as if into the caldera of a volcano. It was a large white male with a ponytail and leather jacket. His ankles were duct-taped and his hands were missing. His arms were adorned with an illiterate and violent manuscript of tattoos. The victim had a bullet hole in the back of his head.

Tony sighed, thinking Amateur Hour. Sheer laziness. He wanted to approach the Don in an attempt to dissuade him from distributing the workload. He had been unable to think of a way to do so without coming across as greedy and/or bloodthirsty, rather than as the consummate professional that he was.

"Poor soul. A tragic accident, it appears to be," Tony said.

"Yes sir, that likewise was my very thought too. He must of wandered in after hours and tripped and fell."

"He is unfamiliar to me. Perhaps a transient?" Tony said.

"Yeah, I never saw him before either. Like you say, he's probably some bum. We get them in here looking for stuff to steal."

In fact, the victim was known to this pair and to many others. Despite rats and maggots beginning recycling processes of their own, he was still recognizable as Buford (Frog Prince) Poe, leader of a biker gang that had formed in prison.

Poe's bulging eyes and flat mouth inspired the nickname. It was derived in childhood from the fairy tale in which a princess kissed a frog, magically transforming it into a handsome prince. In Buford Poe's case, so the joshing went, the transformation had gone haywire in midstream and he'd wound up as part human and part amphibian.

Poe's gang was rumored to be horning into the Ripugnantes' drug action, a practice guaranteed to drastically reduce one's life expectancy.

"It is so unfortunate to be cut down in the prime of life when you lose your footing," Tony said, patting the forklift. "Let's give him a decent burial within the effluvium."

"The what?"

"The noisome hilltop upon which we are standing."

"Yes sir."

"Now."

"Right away, sir."

"Global warming."

4

"Huh?"

"We have done the planet a service by interring the accident victim here. Now your scrap aluminum is unlikely to be contaminated, thus significantly purer. It can be melted and recycled with a fraction of the energy required to smelt it from bauxite ore, thus a concomitant reduction in carbon dioxide emissions."

Chuck looked at him.

At the bottom of the hillock, Tony dismounted the forklift and said, "Do have a nice day."

*****

Dave Pomeroy, beat reporter on the medium-sized city's doomed newspaper, was taking a rare afternoon off at his favorite bar. There were three people in the place, staring at and playing with their tablets, *reading all about it.*

People increasingly got their current events on the Internet, a source as superficial as the summaries read by the talking haircuts on the TV news. Dave wanted to slap the gadgets out of their hands.

Seated on a stool, he drank cold beer from an aluminum can, watching TV. There were no live sports on, so Dave gritted his teeth and contented himself with cable news.

He'd had one or three too many beers when breaking news of an apartment house fire came on. Two persons known dead, two more missing. Arson suspected.

The story brought it all back. When Dave was a child, his favorite aunt perished in an apartment house fire. Probable arson. No arrests. A borderline pyrophobic thereafter, he looked away from the television.

Dave had had an idea from the outset who was responsible for his aunt's murder, but couldn't prove it.

Not yet.

Nor could he bring down the Ripugnantes.

Not yet.

His editor, with nothing to lose that wasn't already being lost, had given David Pomeroy the crime beat and cut his leash.

Dave drained his beer and crushed the can in his hand so loudly that it startled the bartender and caused a customer at the end of the bar to drop his tablet.

2.

ARSENIC. *A metalloid (kind of a semi-metal) with the symbol As; Atomic number 33; Specific gravity 5.727.*

Arsenic combines with other elements to form useful products such as herbicides and pesticides, but it is best known and sensationalized as a killer of humans, intentionally and by accident.

George III of Britain, Simón Bolívar, Napoleon Bonaparte, Clare Boothe Luce, and Francesco I de' Medici succumbed to arsenic in circumstances not entirely clear.

Arsenic was a favorite murder weapon in the Middle Ages. The arsenic-laced cake was a favorite vehicle. Happy birthday; may this be your last.

The symptoms of arsenic poisoning were similar to cholera — headache, severe diarrhea, confusion, vomiting, blood in the urine, cramping muscles, convulsions — a common disease those days.

In Victorian times, women applied arsenic compounds to their faces and arms to improve their complexion and iron out the wrinkles.

Vanity came at a high price.

Madeleine liked to reminisce when she sat on her front porch in her rocking chair, rocking and knitting, a wine glass at her side.

Madeleine's first two husbands died of arsenic poisoning. It was so easy and nobody suspected a thing.

Both men were chronic substance abusers, so who could say what they'd gotten into.

They were macho and then some, as evidenced when they came at her with their fists raised.

Then their health slowly declined.

When the end came, Madeleine was at their bedsides, distraught, inconsolable. There weren't even autopsies.

It was justifiable too, she thought as she touched a forearm scar, the result of being kicked down the stairs by Husband Number One. Thanks to that, she miscarried, never again able to conceive.

Husband Number Two adorned her upper arms with cigarette burns. The clever man, they looked like vaccination scars.

Goodness, could she ever pick them.

Madeleine's magnificently-restored Victorian sat atop a hill directly east of downtown. The city view was semi-spectacular from her front porch. The modest skyline fronted by a Triple-A baseball stadium barely compensated for the foul, dreadful, yellow, Mexico Cityish haze emanating from her left, from Chuck's Waste Management and Recycling. The odor was positively awful when the breeze was wrong, as it was now.

She'd written letters to everybody who could put their foot down with zero response. Since the city was in the pocket of gangsters associated with that hideous landfill, that was hardly an earthshaking surprise.

The only person with the balls to put up a fight against Bruce Ripugnante and his mobsters was a reporter on the city's dying newspaper. The man's editorials read like it was personal. She's emailed him and written via snail mail too. No reply yet, but she held hopes.

Madeleine wondered how long before this Pomeroy individual's crusade ended. One way or the other.

Madeleine continued rocking in her chair, knitting whatever the hell she was knitting. It looked like fuzzy vomit, but no matter, the concept of an old lady rocking and knitting was essential to maintain. She ran a tongue over a lower bridge that replaced teeth lost after a haymaker thrown by the second of two mean drunks she had joined in holy matrimony.

Husband Number Three was a different breed altogether. One and Two were blue collar, a millwright and stevedore respectively. She went white collar the third time around, thinking that he'd be less harmful to her health.

Hah!

Talk about jumping from the fire into the frying pan.

She'd say this for One and Two. They held steady jobs, punching the time clocks even with the worst of hangovers.

Three was a bookish little pseudointellectual who went through jobs like poop through a goose. His best, which he held for all of four months, was as a temporary assistant office manager at a temp agency, a glorified clerk.

Madeleine was at her wit's end after Three began going to church with a temp agency colleague. He came home after the third or fourth service and said he'd been "saved".

Great. She could live with that, but not him plastering a REAL MEN LOVE JESUS sticker on the bumper of her classic 450SL and gluing one of those stupid little fishes on the trunk, which she didn't dare pry off for fear of damaging the paint.

Far worse, Madeleine was being poisoned, a reversal of roles that didn't click until her headaches and diarrhea persisted.

Had Jesus instructed Three to do this? Either Him or his church pal, a young man whose sexual orientation and relationship with her husband were highly suspect.

Hereafter, at dessert she would request that Three go into the kitchen to get her a glass of water or napkin. Then she'd switch the cupcakes he had so thoughtfully baked.

The first arsenic poisoning symptom to hit him was confusion, so it was a cinch to slip a sleeping pill into his morning coffee, lead him to the opened oven, get him on his knees, his chin on the door, and turn on the gas.

Madeleine came home from a leisurely grocery-shopping trip and opened the front door to the smell of gas. Terrified, she called 911.

The fire department came promptly, shut off the oven, and gave her the bad news about her husband. Madeleine was guilt-ridden and inconsolable; he hadn't even left a suicide note.

She had carried six-digit life insurance policies on the losers, so the aftermath of each of her three murdered husbands was a pricier home and fatter bank account.

Madeleine was a handsome woman in her sixties with big graying hair, anonymously-pleasant features, and a nice body. She was conventionally attractive to men in her age range. If so desired, further matrimony was not out of the question.

The insipid rocking was making Madeleine's stomach churn. She got up and went inside. Nosy neighbors would suspect she was retiring to watch talk shows, pop psychologists, and other daytime dreck that told you how to live your life. In reality, lunchtime was approaching, time for another glass of toasty Argentinean malbec.

Lan, Spouse Number Four, having been properly trained by Madeleine and by his tyrannical first wife, was doing the breakfast dishes. She could smell their luncheon quiche in the oven. Who in their right mind would throttle a sweetie pie who did the dishes and cooked like a master chef, she thought, refilling her glass?

She was, however, suspicious that he'd never laid a finger on her in anger. All men were brutes. This was a fact.

Mulling the ledger further: Lan was thin and bespectacled, a retired aeronautical engineer. On the plus side, he had rolled over a fat, juicy 401(k). But he was too quiet and no great shakes in the sack.

Lan preferred doing the dishes to a nooner.

Madeleine took a sip, thinking.

3.

BARIUM. *A soft silvery lightweight metal with the symbol Ba; Atomic number 56; Specific gravity 3.51.*

Barium hasn't many practical uses. It's a component in exotic electronics and a steel alloy. It's also used in fireworks to impart a green color.

In the Middle Ages, witches and alchemists were fascinated by "Bologna stones", smooth pebbles containing barium that were found in and around Bologna, Italy. Once exposed to light, they'd glow for years, undoubtedly goblin-powered.

Barium sulfate is the only barium compound widely known. It's introduced to the digestive tract — at both ends — so it can be imaged in search of the unthinkable.

Judith, a career woman of a certain age, was completing her tenth year at the clinic. It was smallish and the most exclusive in town. Anybody who was anybody came here for the best treatment, damn the cost, and a guarantee of absolute discretion.

Her ten-year bell was tolling this coming Friday. She knew not to expect a party after work, drinks and snacks and gag gifts. No black balloons, no blind dates brought in for her benefit, no nothing. Even if Judith had been gregarious, a partier, it simply was not done here. Not at the DCOR (Discretion Clinic for the Obscenely Rich), as Judith and her limited sense of humor privately termed it.

Judith was chief records clerk. She knew why she had been chosen for the promotion from records clerk when the incumbent retired. She fit a comfortable profile: never married, a childless only child, non-drinker, lived with her mother and a succession of cats (currently five), no male friends in years, a social life confined to weekly dinners with Mom and a trip to the ocean with her in the summer. In other words, dependably dull.

Judith double-checked stacks of folders ready for filing. If they weren't in alphabetical and categorical order, the young lady clerk under her would hear about it. Yes she would. The little gal's preoccupation with fashion and boyfriends was no excuse.

As she worked, Judith tingled at the thought of the patient who had been slipped in through a side door, a lumbering hirsute individual. The typical clinic VIP was male, a town dad or a factory owner. Whether his ailment was socially acceptable or not, it wasn't anybody's gosh-darn business.

This particular gentleman made his money and gained his status quite differently than the majority of DCOR patients.

The Don, she heard somebody whisper. The Godfather.

As Judith thumbed through the files, the theme music from that *Godfather* movie playing inside her head, she felt sympathy for the gentleman, as much as she could for so awful a person who was supposedly behind who knows how many murders, not to mention drugs and everything else in town illegal. The poor man was in for a barium cocktail in one end and a barium enema in the other. It had to be beyond serious.

A laundry list of people would love to be informed if Mr. Ripugnante had an ominous health problem, beginning with that crusading newspaperman. The town's paper was getting thinner and thinner, like most newspapers in mid-sized cities, a victim of electrons on screens. He probably had no money to pay for a "scoop" and his days might be numbered too.

Not to be ignored was the reality that gangsters were known to be easily offended.

Judith knew others had a vested interest in this man's health or lack thereof, people willing to pay plenty for it. The district attorney was the safest and she assumed they had a budget too. Business rivals also, making her an offer she can't refuse. They were risky but had oodles of spare cash.

Oh, the possibilities!

No no, let's be practical. You are *not* one to take risks, she reminded herself.

That newspaper reporter. It had to be him. The paper doubtlessly had connections with more prosperous publications, like those tabloids in supermarket checkout lines. Syndication, she believed they called it. There'd be money for her after all.

She felt giddy and her fingertips were numb. She dropped a file on the floor. As she picked it up she realized that this might be her shot, her one chance for fun and adventure.

Judith had wanted to take a cruise for ages, but not the shabby, affordable ones dragging Mom along, spending half their time standing in buffet lines with obese people, but a once-in-a-lifetime trip on a big ship that went through the Panama Canal and visited a hundred exotic places. She'd loosen up, attend parties, meet fascinating sophisticated people, eligible men among them. If something happened it happened.

Mom could take care of herself for a week or three, playing cards and gossiping with the other biddies at the senior center.

Couldn't she?

If only Judith could make up her mind.

"Dithering" is my middle name, she often thought, whether it be letting a boyfriend in her pants (twice long ago, no fun for either her or her partners), accepting a marriage proposal (just once offered and declined, as he was three sheets to the wind, fumbling for her zipper), schooling, career choices, you name it.

It was so much more comfortable to sit on that file.

And think.

4.

BISMUTH. *A brittle metal with a silvery white color and a pinkish hue because of surface oxidation with the symbol Bi; Atomic number 83; Specific gravity 9.78.*

For a heavy metal, bismuth has an unusually low toxicity. It's utilized in cosmetics, pharmaceuticals, pigments, and as a non-toxic substitute for lead.

The most common use is in a pink solution or tablet widely sold for upset tummies.

Two weeks to the day before the inspection of the late Buford (Frog Prince) Poe's tragic accident at Chuck's Waste Management and Recycling, Antonio (Tony Whack Job) Spazento had performed his latest assignment for the Ripugnantes.

A dusky foreigner had ridden into town with a quantity of black-tar heroin and a laissez-faire attitude. Tony arranged a meet, with the ruse of making a substantial buy.

Tony's weapon of choice was a .25 caliber automatic that easily fit in a pocket behind a hankie. In the chamber was a round that Tony had hollowed out until it was nearly translucent. His anchorman persona allowed him to get close enough to the assignment to press it against an ear and fire. The auditory canal was nature's silencer and the slug butterflied, transforming gray matter into porridge.

Tony's last words to him were, "Yo, bro, dude, a wasp's gonna land on your ear. I'll get it,"

That evening, on a deserted farm, behind a rotting barn, whistling while he worked, Tony whacked the Third-Worlder into small pieces with an axe. He thought of the Lizzie Borden rhyme.

Lizzie Borden took an axe.
And gave her mother 40 hacks,
When she saw what she'd done,
She gave her father 41.

Lizzie Borden was Tony's gal pal. Tony had a negligible libido and was not easily aroused by a flesh-and-blood female. When he was in the mood, he masturbated to a picture of serious, homely Lizzie, imagining what was inside that Victorian garb. Muscular yet feminine biceps propelling the axe. A husky torso, firm buttocks, a dense forest of pubic hair.

Whack.

Off with a forearm.

Whack.

Not a tendon dangling. Superb work for a man who did not take an anatomy course in college. Antonio (Tony Whack Job) Spazento, who despite protestations from his family, had obtained a BA in philosophy and an MA in American history. Engineering and physical science majors sneered at them, saying what use are those sheepskins?

Oh, for one, his studies verified the fragility of life. Any semblance of guilt was obliterated by man's inhumanity to man. He worked on such a miniscule scale too and the majority of his assignments ranked no higher on the morality meter than he.

And he'd be quite happy to compare annual incomes with those lower campus nerds.

As he prepared to go off to college, Tony's late father, a neighborhood boss for the Ripugnantes, had asked him who did he think he was, who did think he was better than? Philosophy ain't nothing and history, that's shit that already happened.

Good points.

Upon graduation, he had three career choices. Teach for peanuts at a community college or be a field reporter for a TV station out in the sticks or, thanks to his father's influence, join the Ripugnantes as a "consultant" and see where that led.

Tony picked the last and his father's recommendation to the bosses sealed the deal. "The boy acts like a pussy at times, but he's smart and he's mean as a fucking snake."

Whack. Whack. Whack.

The portions were now manageable. He buried them at random over a quarter acre, no less than two feet deep.

Done and perspiring, glowing from a job well done, Tony slipped out of bloodied boots, gloves and coveralls, and buried them too.

There was nothing like a spot of exercise to work up an appetite and Tony was famished. He drove into town, to his favorite steakhouse. At his favorite table, treated like royalty, Tony tucked into a 12-ounce USDA-prime New York strip, medium rare. He made short work of the green salad and baked potato too, and sopped up the pinkish meat juices with garlic bread.

He patted his flat midsection and proclaimed himself satisfied. A teetotaler, Tony had chocolate cake and a cup of black coffee, thinking of his upcoming wedding and what he could and couldn't reveal to his bride.

It was an arranged marriage, more or less, like they did in India and in other primitive societies. Regardless, there was a limit to candor.

Don Bruce had been acting strangely of late, as if he had a personal problem. It was no time to voice reservations to him about the union or stall for time. That Tony was no lady's man was a secret he wished kept.

Bad Elements

Tony signed the check that would never be paid and walked out and around the corner to his Cadillac. Just as he opened the driver's door, he stepped on something squishy.

It was a slug, a flattened gooey slimy slug.

Oh yuck!

Tony gagged and slid into the car, reached into the glove box for a pink tablet, and chewed it just in the nick of time.

5.

CADMIUM. *A soft bluish-white metal with the symbol Cd; Atomic number 48; Specific gravity 8.65. The market for cadmium is shrinking because of toxicity and lithium-ion batteries muscling into nickel-cadmium's market. But cadmium-plated fasteners in aircraft manufacturing remain in healthy demand.*

As do cadmium yellows, oranges and reds in artist pigments.

Peggy Sue Ripugnante stood back from her easel and squinted. By doing so, she could determine if her color fields were in balance. Not quite. If she could only get a handle on the negative space.

She dabbed a brush on her palette, picking up a dab of cadmium yellow medium. She liked the cad yellows, light, medium and deep. They were powerful and versatile, able to stand on their own, or mixed with blues and reds, covering much of the color wheel.

Peggy Sue was an abstract expressionist. Or as Daddy put it, "Painting something that don't look like nothing". How he said it, as if she wasn't capable of anything but slopping paint on canvas willy-nilly.

He'd conveniently forgotten the banal landscapes and vases of flowers she had done in art classes, for which she had won straight A's. Some, birthday and Christmas presents, hung in Daddy's living quarters and office.

She had chosen abstract expressionism for reasons other painters had, for the freedom to convey whatever she felt nonrepresentationally, an attitude and statement truly her own.

Regardless of artistic disapproval, she was Daddy's little girl. Her only sibling, Bruce Junior, had disobeyed orders and freelanced drugs with bikers. Out on bail paid by Daddy, he was, in the vernacular, on the lam, leaving her father holding a very large bag. Her mother was a bathrobe drunk who drifted about the opposite wing of this fortified Tara.

Essentially, Peggy Sue was his family.

Her work had sold in downtown galleries on its merit, not because she was the daughter of Don Bruce Ripugnante. Peggy Sue really wanted to believe that. She wanted to test that belief by slinging paint at a sheet of plywood, a ridiculous Pollock parody, and see how it'd do. She didn't have the nerve.

Peggy Sue, blended a dot of cad yellow medium with neighboring red, creating a hot orange, her mind wandering to her father. If Daddy had his way, there'd be a new family member. He had done all but arrange her marriage to Tony Spazento, how it was done in South Asia and the Middle East and those other places where they treated women like sex toys.

"It's your life, Honey, your choice, but –"

All she could summon as an argument was a posture as rigid as a statue.

"He been to college and you'd look great on his arm," Daddy had said.

Tony was a looker, no question about that. If he didn't work for Daddy as a "consultant" he could move right into an anchorman's chair. He was nice and polite, too. Peggy Sue had heard disturbing rumors about him as Tony "Whack Job", but couldn't visualize him harming a soul.

He had a manicure and a smile that could land him work doing toothpaste commercials. She chalked it up to jealousy by other members of Daddy's crew.

She had been out to dinner with Tony a couple of times. He'd been a perfect gentleman, although she wished he hadn't. He'd lectured her on wine complexities, but hadn't laid a hand on her. That gave her pause, as did the absence of a lover boy reputation. To put it mildly, albeit crudely, Antonio Spazento should be getting more ass than a toilet seat.

Peggy Sue was no innocent concerning Daddy. Like it or not, she was a "Mafia princess".

Daddy was the city's mobster boss, seemingly untouchable, but one person didn't think so. Dave Pomeroy, the newspaper reporter. Dave Pomeroy, who was as stubborn as a mule.

Daddy seethed at the mention of Pomeroy. He claimed unconvincingly to be a believer "in that Amendment or whatever the hell it was that gave you free speech." The bottom line was that Pomeroy's assassination would be on the front page everywhere. Daddy's free reign in their corrupt little city would end, blitzed by every state and federal law enforcement agency.

Daddy had enough problems, perhaps one more recently, one he refused to talk about. Worrisome too, maybe related to it, he hadn't answered his phone for the past day and a half.

Peggy Sue had seen Pomeroy's picture. He was a looker too, but different than Tony. He was disheveled and intense, with a nose that had been broken playing junior college football, a man not in the least pretty. Tony had his nails done; she'd be willing to bet Pomeroy didn't. As stressed out as he must be, Pomeroy probably chewed his to the quick.

Bad Elements

She couldn't get Pomeroy out of her mind as she squinted again at her canvas. The negative space was totally out of kilter and the painting was too far along to fix.

She drizzled linseed oil on a cloth and wiped the canvas clean.

6.

CALCIUM. *In the pure form a shiny metal with the symbol Ca; Atomic number 20; Specific gravity 1.55. Though the fifth most abundant element in Earth's crust, calcium is rarely seen as an element since it's unstable in air, decomposing quickly into compounds such as calcium carbonate and sulfate and phosphate. It's a major component in teeth and fingernails.*

Compounds that comprise calcium include chalk, gypsum and bone.

Del liked to kid that he'd fooled around with metal detectors since they invented the electric battery. That wasn't far from the truth. The one he was using now was a dandy, with all the extras. The kids and grandkids had chipped in on it for his last birthday.

They made Del promise to stop driving around looking for places to sweep with a can of beer between his legs. He promised, but fingers and toes were crossed.

Beer cans were what he mostly found, that and bottle caps and the occasional coin. He began the hobby when beverage cans were made of steel. On a good day back then, he'd find buffalo-head nickels and once an Indian-head penny.

Now, he was at an abandoned farm, sweeping behind the ramshackle farmhouse, all windows busted and graffiti all over it. The barn was sagging, like you could knock it over with a feather. Del kept his distance.

He stopped. The needle was going apeshit, like it was having a nervous breakdown. He unfolded the entrenching tool he had clipped to his belt. He'd bought it at a military surplus store.

Del dug down a foot. No pay dirt yet, but the needle was still throwing a fit. He took a break, drank the beer he'd brought, and got back to work.

Luckily the soil was soft and loamy, so it was easy going to get a couple of feet down, to get his tool under what was making all the fuss on his metal detector. Up came the skeleton of a hand, wrist and part of a forearm. Maggots were having themselves a pig-out on what flesh was left inside. On it was a shredded shirtsleeve and a wristwatch.

He lurched backward, saying, "Holy dogshit, Delbert!"

Del calmed down and probed his find. The forearm bone had been severed clean as a whistle, like it'd been chopped with a sharp axe. Just last week, Granddaughter Lilith was telling him about her biology class, where bones had a lot of calcium in them, and you need milk and cheese in your diet to maintain healthy bones.

These bones were kind of brownish, not too healthy at all. Del didn't imagine the person's other bones were healthy either. The watch was a cheapo and wasn't ever gonna tell time again. There was an inscription on the back of it: From JLR to LHO.

Del fished the cell phone the kids made him carry out of his pocket. They made the goddamn things smaller and smaller, and what the hell was the problem with putting a rotary dial on them?

He poked a nine and a one and a one, and hesitated. What was the all-fired hurry? The axe murderer was likely out of the neighborhood and long gone. Del was trespassing too. They might try to give him grief on that or maybe even pin the crime on him.

Del had been leery of the gendarmes going on back to stories his grandfather told him when he was a kid. During Prohibition, Gramps made bathtub gin and sold it out the kitchen door. The cops took him in a bunch of times instead of chasing after gangsters who were firing tommy guns out the window of their black Fords, Al Capone and Lucky Luciano and the rest of them.

Speaking of gangsters, ask anybody and they'd tell you the law in this town was in the Ripugnantes pocket. He wouldn't put this hand past them. He'd be walking into a shitstorm.

Del punched zero to see if he could get an operator and the number of the local paper. Their reporter, Pomeranian or whatever his name is, he was the only one who had the gonads to take them on. He'd give the guy a jingle and see if he was interested in some buried bones.

7.

CARBON. *Non-metallic and in most pure forms soft and black, with the symbol C; Atomic number 6; Specific gravity 2.26.*

Carbon is with us every single day. We inhale oxygen and exhale carbon dioxide; plants do the opposite. Carbon monoxide is its evil twin, spewed by gasoline engines.

Carbon is present in coal, peat and oil.

The diamond, of course, is the most prized form of carbon. Formed at incredibly high pressures and temperatures at depths as far as 125 miles in the Earth's mantle, diamonds are not realistically forever, per the advertising slogan, but they can be a nice start.

Convinced that Lan, Husband Number Four had been properly trained, Madeleine grew complacent and voiced minor complaints about his performance of domestic chores.

A dust kitten he missed here, a cobweb there. Brownies too gooey, asparagus underdone.

Lan rebelled one afternoon, after she pointed out a dollop of grease on the stovetop. He slung an oven mitt against a hanging row of copper cookware, causing a muffled gong.

He told his wife that he was good and well fed up doing all the cooking and cleaning while she sat in her rocking chair and knitted and read and drank wine. Henceforth, she'd better damn well pull her weight.

Stunned, Madeleine did not rebut, unable to utter a single word of protest. Number Four was becoming abusive in his mild-mannered way, and his aggression and anger could only escalate.

Here we go again.

Numbly, Madeleine nodded. She went inside and washed out her own wine glass.

By and by, it became obvious that her cooking and cleaning was not up to Lan's standards, but what could he say? He'd asked for it.

Lan suspected that she was retaliating in the bedroom. There was a night when she had back strain from taking dishes out of the dishwasher. And another when she had a persistent cough brought about, so she claimed, when the smoke alarm went off and she removed very-well-done ribs from the oven. They were a fifty-fifty mix of carbon and inedible pork.

Lan wasn't feeling 100-percent either. He was sluggish and had a metallic taste in his mouth.

Madeleine's cooking worsened. She made spaghetti that was crisp and bacon that wasn't.

It was time to put an end to this and return to normalcy, Lan thought. A pleading apology would not do. There was something intractable about Madeleine, something he couldn't quite pin down. She was a holder of grudges that she held behind her eyes, eyes that scared the bejesus out of him when she stared at him that way.

Lan did the smart thing and went to a jewelry store for a peace offering.

He selected a three-quarter carat solitaire ring. Lan offered it to Madeleine in a velvet box on bended knee. She clapped her hands and squealed with delight.

Lan told his bride that the jeweler said the diamond was conflict-free and contained a trace of nitrogen that gave it the yellowish tint.

She was a tigress in bed that night and the metallic taste in Lan's mouth gradually went away.

8.

CHROMIUM. *A silvery, hard, brittle and shiny metal, with the symbol Cr; Atomic number 24; Specific gravity 7.19. Most commonly used in stainless steel, which is 20% chromium.*

In the 1950s and 1960s, American cars were bedecked with chrome-plated bumpers and trim, more chromium in one tail-finned monstrosity than in a current Honda dealership.

To calm his nerves, Del worked on the six-pack he had on the ground beside him as he waited for the newspaperman. That skeleton hand in the ground, it was just plain creepy. Del wanted his business done with the reporter and him the hell out of here.

Onto the property lumbered a massive automobile on the sort Del had not seen in decades. The reporter, Dave Pomeroy, climbed out and slammed the door.

"Holy tailfin! My mom and dad had one of these, a fifty-seven Plymouth Fury."

Pomeroy shook his hand, saying, "Close. It's a family hand-me-down, on the same platform as the Fury, a fifty-seven DeSoto Adventurer ragtop with gold accents on the grille and wheel covers, and big V-eight with twin four-barrel carbs, and push-button tranny. Ever since I started pissing off the local wise guys, I've been keeping this rig in a storage facility and getting around in the paper's pool car, a piece-of-shit Taurus with six digits on the odometer and nothing left on the brake pads. You step on the pedal and it sounds like you're twisting a cat's tail.

"I was cruising around in the Adventurer, stretching its legs when the call was transferred to me. What have you got?"

This Pomeroy, he was taller than Del and half as round. He was intense and talked fast. In jeans and T-shirt, he had careless hair, a pigeon-toed walk, muscles and a nose that probably had a story or two behind it. The reporter looked to Del like he didn't mind mixing it up and could take care of himself. No sir, he was nobody to mess with.

"Down here."

They knelt and Pomeroy said, "How'd you find it?"

"I didn't. My metal detector did. Should I be calling the law?"

"After we leave, yeah, but make it anonymous from a pay phone, if you can find one that hasn't been vandalized. This has the Ripugnantes written all over it. They whacked the guy out and didn't want him telling any tales, alive or dead."

"You and them have personal problems, I hear."

"You heard correctly. It goes beyond journalism and pride."

"They never did anything personal to you, did they?"

"Damn good question."

Using a pen, Pomeroy carefully lifted the watch out.

"Those initials, are they a clue?"

Pomeroy said, "Only is you know who JLR and LHO are. Maybe they're both underground."

They stood up and enjoyed Del's beer in silence, Pomeroy thinking.

"I got it," Dave said, laughing.

He went to the DeSoto, got a camera, shot pics of the discovery, and said, smiling, "Tell me who the initials *could* stand for."

Del shrugged and shook his head.

"Jack Leon Ruby and Lee Harvey Oswald."

"Hey, yeah. I remember that day, when Ruby plugged him. I saw it on TV. Think the trail's gone a little cold on JFK conspiratorials, Dave?"

"It was before my time, but everyone I've talked to who was old enough remembers where they were and what they were doing when they heard about JFK too. Just like with nine-eleven."

Del said, "I was in the sixth grade at recess. Some of us were looking up Mary Lou's dress while she was swinging on the swing set. Can't recall her last name, but I know her panties were pink and she didn't mind us looking. That's when they called us in early to break the news. Me and the other guys, we were pissed."

"Del, like most newspapers, mine is withering on the vine. I'm taking on the Ripugnantes with no help from anyone, but my editor gave me the green light and distanced himself, though leaving any of it out of his editorials. I don't blame him and I do respect him. He has a family and a mortgage, but believes freedom of the press is sacred."

Del said, "I subscribe to your paper. You can have that computer screen shit and those things everybody and his brother hold in their hands they're always looking at."

"Attaboy. You're a dying breed, Del, and we're grateful. That mob has too much power in this town, so I'm going to approach it obliquely, to try to open some eyeballs, and make the Ripugnantes lives miserable."

"Huh?"

Dave Pomeroy zoomed in on the watch back and snapped more pics.

"I never thought I'd stoop this low."

"What do you mean?"

"Tabloid City, man."

9.

COBALT. *A hard, glossy metal with the symbol Co; Atomic number 27; Specific gravity 8.9.*

The main source of cobalt is as a by-product of copper and nickel mining.

It's used as an alloy for hardening steel and as a uniquely-blue pigment.

Peggy Sue Ripugnante had an inspiration to use jagged oil-pastel borders on her latest abstract expressionist painting. Her present set of pencils was becoming a crumbling mess, so she decided to go to buy a new set, plus extra ultramarines and cobalt blues, her colors of choice.

She raised her hand to rap on Daddy's door, planning to ask if he wanted her to bring back a cup of coffee or anything. She didn't know if he was home, but she had to try, knowing he'd say no. Worse, Daddy Cupid would recruit Tony, her betrothed, to accompany her.

Out of the house, she called Daddy's private cell number. It rang and rang.

Daddy had been so quiet and gloomy. Poor dear boozy Mother was off his radar, so it must be business, nothing he'd ever divulge to his little girl.

Peggy Sue drove to a nearby mall and made her purchases in a chain department store where she usually shopped. Its art-supplies department was satisfactory for her present needs.

Peggy Sue stopped at a coffee shop. She bought a latte and an oatmeal cookie, picked up a newspaper, and went to a table. She opened her mouth to take a bite, but the headline kept it open: GRISLY DISCOVERY MADE. JFK CONSPIRACY WON'T DIE. It went on to summarize the conspiracy theories and the Tampa and New Orleans mobsters who might have had a hand in the assassination.

The picture took up half the front page, an icky gross severed skeleton hand with a wristwatch showing Jack Ruby's and Lee Harvey Oswald's initials. Peggy Sue had studied the assassination in history class; it had happened so long ago.

The byline was David Pomeroy's. He'd written that there was valid reason to reopen the investigation. Despite a half-century passing, there was good reason then to suspect criminal organization involvement by crime families ruled by their descendants.

Pomeroy, that brave, reckless cutie-pie. Daddy had had the paper delivered in front of his private entrance every day for the past year or so. She knew he didn't subscribe for the crossword puzzles.

He was going to have a cow.

She crossed her legs, tingling.

*****

Bruce Ripugnante, the Don, the Godfather, was indeed having a cow.

Sitting alone in his room at the clinic, feeling sorry for himself, he held the newspaper like a baseball bat.

He'd made a phone call to Tony Whack, told him to buy a paper, read the headline story, and get back to him. Seething, fidgeting in his chair, Don Bruce Ripugnante wondered what that scumbag reporter was trying to prove.

He had an idea who the hand used to belong to. Pretty fucking sloppy. Unlike Tony Whack.

He knew he'd hurt Tony's feelings spreading the work out, like the Frog Prince Poe job. It was no way to treat a future son-in-law, but any way you looked at it, the hand was gonna be trouble.

Enough already from that fucking reporter. Clip him and everybody in the world would know. He'd be living with the FBI.

Tony called.

"I read the paper."

"One word."

"Yes?"

"Fatal accident."

10.

COPPER. *A soft, ductile, malleable metal that conducts electricity well, with the symbol Cu; Atomic number 29; Specific gravity 8.96. Copper combined with zinc makes brass; with tin, it's bronze.*

Many metals are poisonous, detrimental to one's health. But copper as a trace mineral is essential.

Unbeknownst to many, the common nickel, which looks like nickel, is only 25% nickel and 75% copper.

Call him F.W. Dallas Houston, name unknown to the IRS. That's what he went by. Mr. Houston sported the boots, the 10-gallon hat, the "y'all", the whole package.

It was in the storage locker he'd rented where he was catching trouble from these two hombres, one who was wearing all that froufrou juice. Dressed like a lounge lizard, he looked like he oughta be a game show host.

The other with a flat nose, a gut overlapping down over his belt buckle, no neck, he was holding a Louisville Slugger. That's the one his attention *definitely* was focused on.

Houston had unlocked, walked in, and there they were. Without introductions or formalities, they told him he was going to terminate his lease.

"Whoa. I got me a three-year lease to store this property of mine in this locker. Go check at the desk. F.W. Dallas Houston is on the paperwork, paid in full," he said, cocking his thumb at the pallet. "How'd you just walk in here anyway?"

"What's all these rolls wrapped inside the plastic on this pallet, Tex?" asked No-Neck. "It's the only thing in here."

"Rolls of nickels. I got more out in the truck I'm fixin' to unload in here too."

No-Neck swung the bat. Nickels poured out. "No shit. You got a thing for gumball machines?"

"Hey, you can't do that. You can't —"

The perfumed guy who looked like he had no business here raised a hand. "What is your purpose with these coins, Mr. Houston?"

"Well, a nickel looks like nickel, don't it?"

"Yes."

"Actually, they're only twenty-five percent nickel and seventy-five percent copper. Irregardless, face value of the metals is over and above five cents and is growing over and above storage costs."

"A wise investment, Mr. Houston."

"That's my way of thinking. I travel all around, buying up nickels and storing them confidential-like, waiting for the next big jump in metals prices which can come any old time."

"If I may tender a suggestion, reduce overhead by consolidating your hoarding," said the perfumed swell. "Elsewhere."

"It's not hoarding in my mind. It's —"

"What we're trying to tell you, Tex, is get them the fuck out of here. We need this space."

"They're small units, you know. Not good for much. There's a big old antique car next door and it don't hardly fit. A Packard or something."

"Where are you from?" asked the swell.

"Turpentine Springs, Texas. You take I-Twenty westbound outta —"

The raised hand again. "Quaint. When can you be out of here, you and your nickels?"

"This ain't reasonable and I don't think it's legal neither."

"Arrrgh!" The No-Neck went back to work on the nickels, flailing and howling. They cascaded like the storied Vegas slot machine jackpot.

The lounge lizard said, "My colleague's temper is virtually unstoppable and these quality units are soundproofed. I repeat, when can you be out of here?"

"Gimme a week."

No-Neck paused to catch his breath. Snorting.

"Shall we say twenty-four hours? You and your nickels en route to the great state of Texas."

"Impossible."

"Forty-eight hours. My last and final offer."

"Okay, okay. How do I clean up this mess and move it so quicklike?"

In a batter's position, No-Neck said, "You wanna be a ground-rule double, fuckstick?"

Houston took a step backward, slipped on nickels, and fell.

"You are kee-reckt. I will find me a way."

11.

FLUORINE. *A highly-reactive yellow gas with the symbol F; Atomic number 9: Specific gravity 1.336.*

Major practical applications are refrigerant gases, toothpaste and non-stick cookware coating.

Most controversially, fluorine is added to water supplies to retard tooth decay.

Visiting hours at the maximum-security wing of the state pen were strict.

The man outside was on time. So was the man inside, who had no other obligations.

The pair was separated by thick clear plastic and spoke on telephones. Both men were grossly overweight. They wore their hair in ponytails and had a crude gallery of tattoos. The stupidity and terror in the visitor's bodily artwork included swastikas.

"What's going on?" asked the man inside.

"Frog Prince, he ain't been seen."

"Them fucking wops."

"That's what we're thinking too. Buford just up and vanished. It ain't like him. There was plenty on his plate."

"There's enough to go around for everyone, the greedy fucking dagos."

"If Buford don't turn up, you're running the show, you know."

"Hell of a bunch I can do from in here."

"I'll take your orders, pass 'em along. They'll know you're giving me the word."

"What's this shit I hear that was in the paper?" asked the man inside. "Killing some dead president, on account of initials being the same."

"Some dipshit reporter, just trying to sell some papers is all it is. He's been stirring things up."

"That picture they took, that skeleton hand and the watch around it, that watch."

"What about it?"

"The crazy drunk bitch. You know, you can't trust none of them. This one was the worst. She'd get wild-ass drunk and flip for no reason. Me and her, we broke up, after she tried to hit me over the head with a beer bottle. I flung the watch she give me for my birthday, flung it across the room. JLR to LHO. Jane L. Richards to Larry H. Olson, I wonder if this dead guy she gave it to next, I wonder if he had my initials too."

"Couldn't say."

The inmate leaned forward and lowered his voice. "Help me get out of here before it's too late. Fluorine. Fluoride. Fluoridation. Water fluoridation. Fluoridation of our water in here."

"Huh?"

"Believe it."

"Sapping our vital bodily fluids is what they're doing, like they did in this old black-and-white movie with a crazy general who tries to start a nu-cu-ler war where the world blows up in the end, except this is for real."

"It is?"

"They do it in here to keep us calm and behaving."

"It ain't working."

"You don't know it's working, but it is. Hitler used fluoridation too, to make everyone stupid and like sheep."

The visitor scratched the swastika tattoo on his forearm, looked at his watch, and said, "We're about out of time."

"Don't believe me, do you?"

"I'm not in, you know, your situation no more. The water I drink, I don't know if it's got fluoride in it or not."

The prisoner stood. "You take the story to that reporter. He'll blow the lid clean off it."

"I will," said the man outside, thinking *sure I will.*

12.

GOLD. *A yellow, lustrous, crazy-making metal with the symbol Au; Atomic number 79; Specific gravity 19.3.*

Since forever, gold has been avidly sought after for coinage and jewelry. Monetary policies have been set around gold and nations still hold large quantities of it – i.e. Fort Knox.

All the gold ever found would fit in two Olympic-sized swimming pools. That doesn't discourage people from chasing after more, in many ways, legally or illegally.

Dave Pomeroy didn't bring a cameraman along to the convenience store because the owner said he'd interview, but, please, no photos. Dave carried a pocket camera just in case he changed his mind.

Mr. Singh, Dave thought, was thoroughly sick of the attention, but didn't mind the extra business. When you sell a winning $690 million lottery ticket, people line up to buy the next winner. That's akin to keeping a book on roulette numbers, but the paper's story wasn't to be regarding luck, it was the two weeks without the winning ticket being turned in and the prize claimed.

Rumors abounded.

1. The ticket was forgotten and lost in a laundry load, two-thirds of a billion bucks worth of paper pulp.

2. A senior citizen had it on the table beside his rocking chair, a ring on it from his glass of prune juice, clueless.

3. And the sexier ones, like the winner who was lining things up: a private jet, bean counters, a precious metals broker, a Caribbean realtor. He'd immediately convert the $690 million into gold, which was climbing again, and away he'd go, leaving behind job and wife.

Dave Pomeroy didn't know what to think when he entered the convenience store. He stood in line by an aisle filled with chips and crackers and candy as the clerk sold lottery tickets, cigarettes, beer and unhealthy, overpriced groceries. Mrs. Singh was at the cash register, he presumed. But where was Mr. Singh and why did she look frightened?

When it was his turn, Dave identified himself.

"Is mistake," she said. "No interview."

"He and I talked only a while ago, ma'am. May I speak to him?"

She shook her head. "Busy."

"May I at least say hello?"

"No. Busy out back."

A conflicting answer which Dave took to mean yes.

Dave walked out back to a fenced-in kiosk that held garbage containers. The man he took to be Mr. Singh was short and dark. He wore an apron and a terrified expression.

He was having an unfriendly conversation with two men, shaking his head. Each boasted gold of their own — necklaces and pinky rings. One had a flat nose, Popeye arms, and no neck. The other was twice his size, but softer looking.

"Am I interrupting something?"

No-Neck turned to him. "Mind your own fucking business, Slick. This is between us and this Arabian."

Dave spread his hands. "It is my business, becoming more so as we speak."

"Get lost. This is private."

Dave smiled, flexing his fists. "I am a member of the fourth estate, swaddled by the First Amendment."

"Lemme show you to your car, Slick," No-Neck said, coming out of the kiosk, an index finger extended. His partner trailed, casting a shadow.

"Do not touch," Dave said, standing fast. "I repeat, do not touch."

No-Neck touched, a hard jab to the chest with the extended finger.

"Fuck your do-not-touch. I ain't gonna tell you ag — "

Dave took the finger with both hands and shoved backward. No-Neck screamed as a knuckle snapped and he slammed into the fence. He dropped to his knees. Howling, he started to get up, but Dave put a knee below his jaw and he dropped again.

Dave backed off and put up his dukes. "If you want to fight clean, do it the Marquess of Queensberry way, I'll let you up."

No-Neck spit out a tooth and glared homicidally. He spit out another tooth.

Dave waited.

Drooling blood, he didn't move.

Dave looked at the other one. He had beady eyes, eyebrows that were a single row, and three chins. He didn't move either. If this wasn't a Ripugnante crew, he was Snow White.

"Get your buddy out of here."

As the larger goon assisted the muttering No-Neck to his feet, Dave aimed his camera. "Smile."

When they were gone, Mr. Singh said, "Please go. Too much trouble."

"You'll be page one tomorrow, sir. They won't be able to touch you. What were they after?"

"They believe I remember who bought that ticket. If I didn't say, they would help my memory with their fists."

"*Do* you remember?"

"No no. Even before the big winner, I sell hundred of tickets a day. Now thousands and thousands. How can I remember?"

13.

HYDROGEN. *The lightest and most abundant element, from which so much derives, with the symbol H; Atomic number 1; Specific gravity .00009.*

Thermonuclear fusion, the transformation of hydrogen to helium, ignites the hydrogen bomb and keeps the sun burning.

Hydrogen is in numerous substances worth killing one another over, including water and petroleum.

Brady had sold refrigerators to Eskimos. Space heaters and electric fans too. He worked at an Anchorage appliance store before they caught his hand in the till and on the owner's wife, and gave him the heave-ho.

Penny ante anyhow, he thought on his way out of town.

Drifting from one low-rent hustle in the Lower 48, he read newspapers, watched the news, and kept eyes and ears open in search of a fresh angle.

Then he had a vision.

Lobbyists were prominent in the news and not in a good way. Consultants were a subject of outrage also, taxpayer dollars having gone to them for researching some special-interest thing or another.

But they still operated and prospered, skimming the cream off the top.

Brady regarded lobbyists and consultants as brethren. He aspired to membership in that pantheon.

He could easily pass himself off as one of them. All Brady required was an instrument of value. He became fascinated with commodities. Their values roller-coastered. This attracted risk takers.

Brady had settled in a mid-sized city that was reputed to have an exceptionally-strong Mob influence. This was good. It'd encourage self-discipline, not his strong point. He could be reckless if easy money was within reach, so knowing that there were toes he dared not step on was a restraint.

Of the commodities, oil was in his estimation the hottest ticket. People howled (especially SUV owners) when gas had exceeded three bucks a gallon, denouncing domestic oil execs and the OPECers. It was cheap now, but who could say next year or the year after?

Caroming from swanky bars and lounges in the best hotels, Brady got the word out that as a consultant and hydrocarbon expert, he had profitable foreign connections that could turn a dollar on its ear.

He chose Ecuador as his center of expertise, using the Internet to learn it thoroughly. The South American country was obscure, the smallest producer of the OPEC nations. Most visitors were tourists, who went directly to the Galapagos Islands, and knew little of the nation otherwise.

Brady didn't find his prime sucker, he let the prime sucker find him, the way it was done by the pros.

It happened a mere ten days into his campaign. Side by side on barstools, they struck up a banal conversation: sports, the weather, and politics, letting his mark segue into petroleum supply and demand.

The sucker invited him to dinner at the best Italian restaurant in town. They ate in a corner of the lounge, not saying much, letting things develop.

Kind an odd little guy, Brady thought, now in brighter light. Pinstripes that had to cost in the four figures. Wide rimless glasses. Hair combed from where it grew to where it didn't. The rock in his pinkie ring had to be six carats.

"You travel to Ecuador often?"

Brady said, "I do indeed. Ecuador is Spanish for 'equator'. The sun is straight up and down. I burn easily, so I've really gone through the sunscreen on my trips there. Nonetheless, I've fallen in love with Ecuador. The people, the around-the-clock warmth, the cultural aspects, and most of all the business opportunities."

Fair-skinned, with a high forehead, Brady *did* burn easily. The rest was a lie. He'd never been there and never intended to go. It was the Third World, for Chrissake. He'd risk intestinal disorders from the food and water, and attacks by street thugs. Get real!

"You implied that these connections of yours are important, that they help get things done, get investment dollars in the best places."

Brady smiled and rubbed thumb against forefingers. "In that part of the Hemisphere, in the oil industry, money does speak volumes. I'm afraid that things aren't as transparent as they are here, so you do what you have to do."

"An investment, then."

Leaving it there.

"A sound one. There is a finite amount of fossil fuel in the ground and people won't get out of their cars," Brady lectured. "Prices may fluctuate, but they'll eventually go up permanently."

"For a faster upturn."

Brady smiled. "Yes, as I've said, Ecuadorian oil is nationalized, but there are ways of buying and selling locally that increase short-term return. My Ecuadorian associates and I keep that — pardon the pun — lubricated."

His companion didn't smile. He hadn't smiled all evening. And come to think of it, if he gave his name, Brady had forgotten it.

"Our assets will be liquid, you have said?"

"Nothing is more liquid than cash. I can't guarantee anything, but twenty percent return per annum is attainable."

"Our investment capital, when we need any or all, it's there for us?"

It dawned on Brady. They cared not about Ecuador and hydrocarbons. They were laundering money.

"Absolutely, sir."

"Very well. There is a valise with cash for you, under your driver's seat."

Driver's seat of his car, parked under a streetlamp, locked, alarm set. A mountain range of goosebumps erupted on his arms.

The man nodded at their waiter. The check came.

He said, "I'll take care of this. You'd better be on your way and make airline reservations."

In his car, Brady felt the soft valise, and drove home. Inside, he opened it up. There were new hundreds in wrappers, stacks of them."

He poured a straight shot and drank.

Some dribbled on his chin as he wondered who the hell he was working for.

14.

IODINE. *Fairly friendly stuff with the symbol I; Atomic number 53: Specific gravity 4.94. In iodized salt to prevent goiter.*

Once upon a time, a prisoner was said to have carved out a potato in the shape of a small pistol, painted it with iodine to give it a purplish-gun metal color and bluffed his way to freedom, then lighting out in a stolen jalopy. True or apocryphal?

Tincture of iodine was once widely used as a disinfectant. It still is, but not as commonly.

DAVE POMEROY: Madeleine, Dave Pomeroy. Sorry taking so long getting back to you, but your letter got buried in a pile on my unruly desk and I don't check email like I should.

MADELEINE: Oh thank you, Mr. Pomeroy. I'd almost given up.

DAVE: It's Dave. I appreciate your concern.

MADELEINE: Thank goodness somebody cares! When the wind blows from that Chuck's junkyard in our direction, it's almost unbreathable. It's an eyesore too and my eyes feel like I squirted iodine in them.

DAVE: Yeah, everybody in town smells it when they burn rubbish.

MADELEINE: What can you do? Everybody says that it's owned by gangsters and nobody can do a thing.

DAVE: I'll be looking into it. You wrote that you have a good view of Chuck's Waste Management and Recycling.

MADELEINE: Unfortunately we do. The disadvantage of living in view property is that you see the bad with the good.

DAVE: You can help.

MADELEINE: How?

DAVE: If you have time, keep an eye on the thing for me.

MADELEINE: I'm retired and have the time, and I'd love to play private detective. What should I look for?

DAVE: I don't know. Anything you think is suspicious.

MADELEINE: Cool. I'll watch day and night.

DAVE: Outstanding. I'll give you my private number.

MADELEINE: Can you supply me infrared goggles or whatever they are that let you see after dark?

DAVE (laughing): I sure wish I could, Madeleine, but we can barely pay our light bill.

*****

Peggy Sue Ripugnante wondered if she should be fashionably late. The bar was thirty miles out of town, so that'd be hard to judge. She pulled into the parking lot two minutes early. Ninety seconds later, he parked beside her Porsche SUV in a Taurus with squealing brakes that had seen better days. And years.

He got out first and walked to her. He was carrying a manila envelope.

"Nice," Dave Pomeroy said, appraising her vehicle.

"If this is an interview, I've said all I have to say. Reaching me through a gallery owner was clever. Sneaky."

"I'm a reporter. I probe, I research. I am sneaky. They're anxious to do a one-person show with you. Best of luck in that. Have you always been an abstract expressionist?"

"Is there something wrong with that?"

58

He held the car door open for her. "Don't be defensive. I like color, how you use it. I like op art the most. If there was a Victor Vasarely fan club, I'd be president. I have reproductions hanging in my apartment."

Thinking this was like an invitation to see his etchings, she didn't reply.

They went inside and took a table. Each ordered the house red.

"I'm sure you'll get around to telling me what's in that," Peggy Sue said, touching the manila envelope.

"I will. Want lunch?"

"Not yet."

"It's something somebody tried to sell me and the paper."

"You bought?"

"I didn't. I told the person that the paper had no budget for anything. I read the individual the riot act too."

"She just gave it to you? Or did you say he?"

"I didn't say. The person realized it was the wrong thing to do. And stupid. I said, why don't you just walk across a minefield? It'd come back to you regardless how I tried to shield your identity."

"That's the end of it?"

"The person is taking a leave of absence and moving in with a maiden aunt two times zones away."

Peggy Sue drank most of her wine. "I'm getting the impression that you can be as mean and dirty as Daddy's people."

Dave shrugged. He had seen photos of Peggy Sue Ripugnante, a woman with Italianate features, a woman who knew what she wanted in life. Up close, there was a fragility, a porcelain quality that did not run in the family.

"Did you happen to put one of Daddy's goons in the hospital?"

"I am a journalist. I am a defender of free speech as well as myself, and I dislike bullies."

"My innocent ears pick up shards. There's a ninety-thousand dollar estimate on fixing his teeth."

Dave told the lottery-ticket story. "I advised him not to touch me. He touched."

A second round of wine arrived.

"Can I guess what's in the envelope?"

"If you guess it's your father's recent medical records, you're right."

She looked at him.

"He went into a clinic for lower tract testing. I can't read doctorese and all I know about medicine is iodine and a bandage for a cut and how they set a broken nose, but they found polyps. He has to go back in for a colonoscopy. It might not look wonderful for him. They won't know until it's done."

She pressed a fist against her mouth.

He took her free hand and said, "Peggy Sue, listen. This is yours. We're not a *National Slime Bucket* check-stand tabloid. We don't play that way. I'm not being sanctimonious, but I don't believe in this kind of dirty pool. I'd be dragging myself and the paper down to the level of who I'm investigating. As you probably know, I'm not above a tabloid stunt, but nothing like this."

She squeezed his hand and her eyes glistened.

"I still intend on bringing your old man down, but I'll do it my way, exposing him for what he does, not for a medical problem."

After thirty seconds of silence, they picked up their menus.

Neither was very hungry. They had salads and more wine.

"I don't know what to think of you," she said, finishing her wine. "You and that JFK thing for one."

"I don't know what to think of me either."

"Do you have a steady girl?"

"No."

"If you had many girlfriends, I wouldn't be surprised."

"I try to be promiscuous, but it hasn't worked out lately."

"Why not?"

"I'm obsessed with the Ripugnantes. It takes time and I'm dangerous to be around."

"Why your crusade? It sounds personal."

"Part of it is personal, maybe, a part that goes way back, but I'm not going into it. Boyfriends?"

"Nobody steady, although Daddy wants me to."

"Anybody in particular?"

"I'm not going into it."

"More wine?"

Peggy Sue looked at him. "You've gotten women half looped and seduced them."

"Is that a question?"

Peggy Sue studied her wine glass.

"I'm definitely not above that," he said.

She took a deep breath and looked at him. "Did you notice that tacky motel on our right, five miles back, painted in pinks and purples?"

"I did. The 'vacancy' sign was lit."

"Are you reading my mind?"

"I am. I don't want to stay for dessert either."

15.

IRON. *A grayish metal in widespread use since, well, The Iron Age, with the symbol Fe; Atomic number 26; Specific gravity 7.874.*

The 4th most abundant element in earth's crust, iron was the first practicable metal in modern weaponry.

Iron-rich foods like meat, eggs and leafy green vegetables stave off iron deficiency anemia.

Countless tons of usable steel are lost due to conversion to iron oxide, another name for rust.

Over 1500 million tons of steel is produced annually worldwide, in a multitude of applications.

The spring-steel bedsprings in Unit 201 of Tom & Geri's Rosebud Motel squeaked rhythmically much of the afternoon. During interims, the couple held hands and kissed and caressed while their batteries recharged.

Neither had to say that it was going to be more than sex.

~ ~ ~

The man with a flat nose and no neck ate lunch through a straw, enraged that he had to. Thinking homicide, he sat as a colleague worked. They were in a self-storage unit next to the one they'd taken over from the Texan.

His colleague was regarded by the organization as its expert on "iron", their term for cars and any other machinery worth stealing. He had learned auto mechanics in a prison vocational program designed to prepare him for a career on the outside, to prevent recidivism.

Only the colleague's lower legs and feet were visible, for he was underneath a 1957 DeSoto Adventurer on a dolly, with a portable light, tools tapping and clattering.

"He's as good as dead," he said when he rolled out.

"An accident?"

"There won't be nothing left to say one way or the other."

~ ~ ~

Don Bruce Ripugnante had made an appointment for the procedure and was back home. He sat in the dark, watching his favorite movie. He couldn't get his mind off what had to be done, bent over, his feet in steel stirrups as a doctor went at him with some kind of thing like you cleaned kitchen pipes with.

He remembered how Albert Anastasia, boss of Murder Incorporated, got whacked in 1957. In for a shave, helpless too in the barber's chair, towel over his face, something he did every single day.

Bruce would be totally helpless too. If somebody busted in and whacked him out, it'd be degrading, the story all over the news. He'd never live it down.

He didn't know what the hell to do.

Do it or not?

Don Bruce Ripugnante's favorite part of the movie was on.

Puffing out his cheeks, he spoke along with Brando.

I'm gonna make you an offer you can't refuse.

~ ~ ~

Across the highway from Tom & Geri's Rosebud Motel, in a ratty strip mall, parked in front of a payday loan outfit his bosses had a piece of, a man watched and waited.

Inside his jacket was a nine-millimeter Glock that held seventeen rounds. In his hand was a Sony DSC-HX200V. It had an 18.2 megapixel sensor and a 30X zoom lens.

Wherever she went, he went — orders of the Don.

He watched and he waited.

The Don, he wasn't gonna be happy.

16.

LEAD. *A soft, malleable, toxic metal with the symbol Pb; Atomic number 82; Specific gravity 11.34.*

Used in car batteries, radiation shielding, bullets, glass, movable type, and, formerly, plumbing pipe, gasoline and alchemy.

"Lead poisoning" has multiple definitions, with overlapping innuendoes.

Iggy, age 39 1/2, lived in his mother's basement. The old lady had fully furnished it to keep him there, under her thumb.

Iggy had bought the $690 million lottery ticket.

He bought a lottery ticket every day from the convenience store around the corner from their dilapidated house, where he selected his dinner entrée of chips and candy. He bought it from Mrs. Singh or her husband or a cousin. They all had Singh on their nameplates. He couldn't tell those A-rabs apart, any of them.

He lived with his mother and her current husband, the fourth or fifth. This husband's employment record was every bit as spotty as most of the others, so she was preparing to unload him.

Iggy was pear-shaped and had a yellow keyboard of rotting teeth. He was batshit loony, unemployable at every level and dangerous to himself and others. He talked to himself and he bayed at the moon. He refused all medication, claiming that communists wished to use drugs to extract atomic secrets from him.

But he wasn't stupid and had periods of lucidity. After he saw the winning number in the following day's paper, Iggy ran upstairs and told Mommy, pleading with her get the divorce papers signed and get the husband the hell out of there before he turned in the ticket, which he finally did, requesting and receiving anonymity that proved to be temporary.

Iggy took a $331 million lump sum. Iggy's mommy was beanpole-thin with a gray beehive and skin prematurely wrinkled from chain-smoking. After a stop at a clinic to buy herself a set of silicone tits, she immediately went on an around-the-world cruise, ready, willing and able to make her next mistake in the choice of a member of the opposite sex.

After Iggy had the house to himself, he hired a security firm to keep watch on the main floor and chase off unwelcome visitors, of which he now had many. When you're $331 million richer, a flock of the long-lost try to reenter your life. Women who crossed to the other side of the street when they saw him coming made marriage proposals. A third of a billion bucks had made him as handsome and dashing as a Hollywood leading man.

The basement was home sweet home anyway. A barrier to the unwanted in place, Iggy, a frustrated inventor, went to work. Never before did he have the funds to tackle anything.

Now he could take on *anything*.

Alchemy.

Iggy was going to change lead into gold and be the richest dude in the whole wide universe.

~ ~ ~

Josh, Dave Pomeroy's editor, sat alone in his office, in the dark, drinking straight bourbon from a water glass.

The hard-boiled, hard-drinking newspaper editor was a cliché, so why not enjoy? Do what you're expected to. Tomorrow morning's edition had been put to bed and everybody had gone home.

Josh refilled his glass and looked out at the city room and its glowing computer screens.

The glow used to be a constellation, now fast becoming a black hole. A great metaphor for the novel he'd never gotten around to writing.

At least no pink slips came down from the brass this week, thank God.

He thought back to the days when he was breaking in. Of lead slugs and ink smeared all over his hands when he set type. Josh's first editor expected his cub reporters to know the business from soup to nuts.

All in the past, a past that had been murdered by electrons.

He thought of Dave, a lone wolf with fangs, how he'd turned him loose, given him carte blanche on the Ripugnantes.

He drank, hoping he hadn't handed Dave a death sentence.

A posthumous Pulitzer was no consolation.

17.

LITHIUM. *A soft, silvery-white, unstable featherweight of a metal with the symbol Li; Atomic number 3; Specific gravity 0.535. Used in lithium-ion batteries, lithium grease, and lithium carbonate pills to treat mania and bipolar disorder.*

Lithium serves no obviously vital biological function. Therefore, it's not in multivitamin tablets.

Bolivia has over half the world's lithium and makes sure everybody knows it does.

"Mother, are you supposed to drink when taking your lithium medication?"

Holding a champagne flute, Madge Ripugnante listed slightly to starboard.

"I alternate. Drink, medicate, drink, medicate. Perfectly safe and sane."

Peggy Sue Ripugnante said, "Please, Mother, sit down. We have to talk. I need your advice."

Her mother made a soft landing beside her on the sofa, spilling nary a drop of her fizzy orange drink that Peggy Sue knew to be a mimosa. Madge's bathrobe was clean too. Considering her alcohol consumption, these were minor miracles. But for the broken capillaries, she'd keep her looks too and gravity hadn't claimed much of her hourglass figure - a *major* miracle.

"A meaningful talk?"

"Yes, meaningful."

"That's what a mother's for, Dear."

They hadn't had a heart-to-heart for eons. The request seemed to sober her. Slightly.

"I think I'm in love."

Madge put her mimosa on her end table and squeezed her daughter's hands. "That's wonderful! Is it somebody in the art community?"

"No. This man is Daddy's worst enemy."

"A rival?"

"No. He's the newspaper reporter who's bound and determined to destroy the Ripugnantes. Daddy will have a cow if he finds out we're lovers."

"Oh, don't you worry, Dear. If he was a rival, he'd have him killed lickety-split, but he can't kill a reporter. It'd be the world's biggest story and your daddy would fall like Humpty Dumpty."

"I feel better. I think."

"Don't get me wrong. Your daddy is not a nice man. Even though I'm in exile here at home, I know more than anybody realizes."

Peggy Sue Ripugnante considering telling her that her daddy was a very sick man. But she said nothing.

Madge Ripugnante held up her glass. "Hmm, I'm running on empty. May I fix you one too?"

Hungover and blissfully sore, Peggy Sue said, "Yes, please."

~ ~ ~

Of course Brady hadn't gone to Ecuador as promised, taking care of oil business for his investor/money launderer. He went instead to Vegas on a three-day gambling and whoring bender, of which he recalled little.

Home now, head aching and stomach queasy, fiddling on the Internet, he came across a piece on Bolivia. With the demand for lithium surging, it was becoming known as the Saudi Arabia of Lithium.

Bolivia wasn't all that far from Ecuador.

It'd be an easy side trip on the next trip he wasn't going to take.

18.

MERCURY. *Silvery, glossy, pretty, mesmerizing and deceptively nasty stuff that melts at -38° F, with the symbol Hg; Atomic number 80; Specific gravity 13.534.*

There are industrial applications, but because of toxicity, mercury is in decreased use in thermometers and dental amalgam.

It accumulates in critters too, notably seafood, not a good thing. Mercury can kill you many different ways.

Hard at work in his basement, lead melting in a crucible above a burner, repelled by photos emailed by his mother of lean and tanned young men at Biarritz, where she was wasting no time spending her concept of quality time. Iggy wondered what next. She'd scrapped her cruise-ship plans and flown there nonstop, dealing with jet lag with post-teen debauchery, the old slut.

Available texts on lead-to-gold alchemy went back centuries and were no help. Without exception, they concluded that it could not be done. *Pb* to *au* was impossible.

Iggy was just about ready to give up, eat a candy bar, and take a nap when he began receiving radio contact through his fillings. A steady line of signals came through his left lower molars, the mercury compound packing holes in his rotting teeth being the precise frequency.

Over the years, this was where Iggy received the most powerful and assertive messages. He never told a soul. They'd misunderstand and think he was crazy.

The planet Mars was the origin of the transmissions.

How could it not be?

Look and listen, one and all! Mars has a thin atmosphere that was once thick. It had running water that came up to the knees. Its axial tilt and length of day are similar to Earth's. Its gravity is 38% of ours. It's cold, but not that cold, not like Saturn or Neptune. But you'd dress warmly if you had an ounce of common sense.

Iggy bounced on his toes. On Mars, it'd be the world's record in the high jump.

Bouncy, bouncy.

Martians took interest in us when we took interest in them. Yes, they certainly did, trailing and sniffing after the probes and rovers we sent there.

Iggy wrote furiously as they advised him how to proceed. Once he became the richest dude in the world and he became emperor, he'd have a summit conference with their grand bwana. They'd meet on our moon or Deimos or Phobos. Details to be worked out later.

Iggy pounded on the ceiling with a broom and yelled. He went up the basement steps, met the director of security at the door, and gave him his latest shopping list.

The security director handled all his needs.

A nice man, almost fatherly.

Iggy had instantly distrusted him.

19.

NEON. *An inert, odorless, colorless gas with the symbol Ne; Atomic number 10; Specific gravity .0009.*

Used in signs, vacuum tubes, and lasers.

"Neon-hued" clothing was back in fashion.

To many it defines glamour and glitz: NYC's Times Square, Miami's South Beach, Las Vegas.

In the middle of the night, Brady's phone rang. He fumbled for it on the nightstand.

WOMAN: Bradykins?

BRADY: Uh, er, yeah.

WOMAN: This is the Neon Queen.

BRADY: Who?

WOMAN: From Vegas, Bradykins. My neon-colored short-shorts and panties and halter-top. You named me The Neon Queen. That was so so so so so so adorable of you.

BRADY: I think maybe you have the wrong number.

WOMAN: No I don't, Bradykins. You tossed money around like those whales the casinos fly in from Asia to lose at baccarat. You didn't play cards. You shot off your mouth.

BRADY: I did?

WOMAN: Yes you did. You are *so* smart, the way you hustled gangsters out of money, making them believe you were going to Ecuador to invest their money in oil, then feed it back to them a little at a time, like, you know, one of those Ponzi things. It was so complicated, so awesome, you patted me on the head, understanding that I barely understood a word, me being, you know, a Vegas bimbo.

BRADY: (barely audible groan).

WOMAN: I'm used to guys treating me like that. You know, like a Barbie doll with a snatch.

BRADY: How did you get this number?

WOMAN: The Neon Queen. I think about that tag you gave me and the private striptease I did for you with every neon outfit in my wardrobe, every radioactive shade in the rainbow. Do you wish to know who else likes me to do erotic dances?

BRADY: No.

WOMAN: Since you insist, a variety of bad people. Bugsy Siegel may no longer rule this town, but his contemporary counterparts love to visit, among them those you boasted you bamboozled. Bradykins, are you still there?

BRADY: Yeah.

WOMAN: Among others, you may regard me as a dingbat and a whore, and I accept that. I have an MBA from UNLV, but as long as I have my bod and my looks, I'm going to do what I do. It pays much much better than information technology or corporate finance. When somebody like you comes along, it's bonus time. Bradykins, hello.

BRADY: I'm still here.

WOMAN: Do you have pen and paper handy?

BRADY: (fumbling on the end table for pen and paper) I think so.

WOMAN: Good. Take this number down. It's for an offshore account. Transfer fifty thousand to it and you'll never hear from me again.

BRADY: What it I don't, bitch.

WOMAN: Can you say Ri-pug-nan-te?

BRADY: Shit. Gimme a minute to turn on the light and double-check that number.

~ ~ ~

Speaking of Las Vegas:

In an alley, several blocks from Las Vegas Boulevard South, better known as The Strip, a man was on his knees, drunk and bleeding, head against a wall to maintain some semblance of equilibrium.

The man had been escorted out of a casino on The Strip after a clumsy attempt at blackjack card counting.

Unwilling to cut his losses, he had pushed and shoved his escorts, screaming, "Don't you losers know who I am?"

Then he made the mistake of telling them who he was.

Bruce Ripugnante Junior was like his father a large man. But Junior was soft and unintimidating, no matter how hard he tried to play the bully.

Opportunity knocking, the escorts acted on their own, above and beyond their job description. They rolled him a block from his apartment and took everything of value he carried, including keys to his apartment and car, from which they took everything else of value.

In the hospital, getting stitched and his bruised ribs wrapped, Bruce Ripugnante Junior pondered his future. He had been living on what he'd skipped with and by his wits, which was to say that he'd been living on what he'd skipped with.

Unless he thought of something fast, he didn't have a future.

20.

NICKEL. *An attractive silvery color that oxidizes slowly, with the symbol Ni; Atomic number 28; Specific gravity 8.9.*

Corrosion-resistant, nickel is used for plating other metals. German silver is 20% nickel.

And there are the aforementioned coins in one's pocket and purse.

Dave Pomeroy sat in his editor's office for his reminiscence/lecture. Once a monthly ritual, it was closer now to weekly.

No matter how pissed at him Josh was, Dave knew he was still the teacher's pet.

The editor opened a desk drawer, and took out a bottle of whiskey and two glasses, how it was done in the movies. He poured two shots, fished a nickel out of his pocket, tossed it on his desk, and said, "I can remember when a paper cost this much."

They'd started off like this before, not with a nickel but something obscure and dreamy. Josh had had a belt or two already.

"The good old days."

The editor lifted his glass and sipped. Dave did the same.

Josh was old. His tie was older than Dave Pomeroy.

"Not always the good old days, though. I'll say this, back then the printed word wasn't dying and a paper was twice as thick as it is now for seventy-five cents or a buck. Christ, two dollars for the Sunday edition that went for a quarter."

"Uh huh," Dave said, wondering if it was a question.

"The advertising has jumped ship to those little pixels on a screen."

"It has," Dave said. "Yes it has."

"The last couple of days, we've sold papers. The machines ran out here and there." He checked a printout on his desk. "We picked up 147 new subscribers too."

"Good," Dave said, knowing where this was going.

"Reopening the JFK assassination, you can't be serious."

Dave shrugged. "I'm not, Josh. Not necessarily. That watch, those initials. Maybe, maybe not."

"I got an email from a math prof. He did permutations and combinations and all that mathematical stuff on those six initials. Jack Leon Ruby and Lee Harvey Oswald came up umpteen kazillion to one."

"Can I use that?"

"No."

"I'm rattling cages is all, Josh. To see if anyone will step forward."

"One of the three tramps on the Grassy Knoll?"

"Whomever. It might lead to facts on the severed hand."

"Hands. You know I gave you a free hand on the Ripugnantes. If the paper's going down in flames, he might as well bring those psycho crooks down with us."

"Much appreciated."

"Please don't go permanently tabloid on us is all I ask."

"I'm going to bring them down."

"Or die trying, goes the saying."

"I'll try not to go too far. Try as hard as I can"

"These people are psychopaths, David. They do cruel things. This is part and parcel of their job description"

"I guarantee I'll hurt someone badly if they attempt to hurt me, Josh."

"You already have at the convenience store."

"Couldn't be helped. I told him not to touch me. He touched."

Dave let his voice trail off. He was within an eyelash of telling Josh about Peggy Sue. Josh had been a mentor to Dave. In the past, he'd asked and received matrimonial and professional advice from a man who had been married and divorced three times, a man who had done and seen it all.

The editor picked up the nickel.

"I'm old enough to remember when papers were a nickel. I was probably in grade school when the paper was bumped to a dime. My father was the paper's editor-in-chief then."

Dave said nothing.

"A plug nickel, David. To the Ripugnantes, your life isn't worth a plug nickel."

Dave drank his whiskey.

He had no rebuttal.

21.

NITROGEN. *Seventy-eight percent of the air we breathe, an inert gas with the symbol N; Atomic number 7; Specific gravity .001251. Participates in all sorts of products: ammonia fertilizer, liquid nitrogen, nitric acid.*
Nitroglycerin too.

No-Neck's partner at the convenience store was ordered to do it, no bullshit, no arguing, just do it. This was his reward for being a faggot and a pussy behind the convenience store and not pitching in with the reporter who sucker-punched his partner.

It was nighttime, two blocks from the self-storage facility. He had been carrying the jar in the car and now he carried it oh so carefully from the car where No-Neck sat behind the wheel.

His destination was the reporter's tail-finned antique car. Their mechanic had installed straps on the undercarriage to accommodate the jar. The jar that had been designed to contain home-cooked preserves contained "blasting oil", a mixture of nitroglycerin and gunpowder.

The man with beady eyes, eyebrows that were a single row, and three chins was extremely careful on the sidewalk approaching the facility. There were cracks in the concrete and there were bulges in it from tree roots. He saw and avoided every one of those, but he didn't see the banana peel.

Kaboom

As No-Neck peeled out of there, if he could have spoken clearly through his damaged mouth, he would have eulogized, "Lord rest the dummy's soul if he got one."

~ ~ ~

One of the first detectives on the scene diagnosed the reason why there were body parts scattered in a two-hundred-yard radius. The victim had been carrying an explosive device that detonated prematurely. An avid soccer fan, he described it to his partner as "an own goal."

~ ~ ~

In bed at Tom & Geri's Rosebud Motel, Room 201, before they showered together and went out to breakfast, Peggy Sue and Dave watched the morning news, sound muted. The lead story was a mysterious and deadly explosion and a gruesome death.

"Don't you wish you were there covering that story?" she asked, her hand on him.

"Not now."

"That story. It bothers you, doesn't it, the way you're staring?"

"Not really," he said, a small fib.

What bothered him was the self-storage place in the background, less than two blocks from the blown-out glass, smoking cars, and small crater in the sidewalk.

Suffering a dose of paranoia, Dave went to the window and peeked through the curtains. The car he thought he'd seen before was parked across the street in the strip mall, in front of a payday loan shop.

"What're you looking at?" she asked.

"Just checking the weather."

~ ~ ~

The man in the strip mall monitoring the Rosebud Motel did not see Dave peeking out. To relieve boredom throughout the night, he had been playing on his tablet a series of violent video games. Now he watched the news feed and its lead story, an unexplained explosion near where the reporter stored his old car.

22.

OXYGEN. *Twenty-one percent of our air, an odorless colorless gas with the symbol O; Atomic number 8; Specific gravity .001429. Used in production of many things. Oxygen reacts with almost anything, forming a kazillion compounds, most annoyingly with iron to become rust.*

Oxygen liquefies at -361.82°F. Liquid hydrogen mixed with liquid oxygen is the quintessential rocket fuel.

Antonio (Tony Whack Job) Spazento was an oxygen-treatment believer. He believed in its therapeutic quality.

This is why he breathed aerosol oxygen and had an oxygen-rich serum treatment to invigorate his facial pores prior to visiting Peggy Sue and popping the question.

The oxygen salon was right around the corner from where he had his nails done. Arranged marriage or otherwise, it was his job as the man, the prospective bridegroom, to look his very best when he asserted his wishes.

He'd had a lovely four-carat stone taken from a pinky ring reset in a gold filigree style. The former owner had no further use for it. Tony thought it'd be advantageous to bone up on nonrepresentational art, her love. The end result of Tony's work was akin to Picasso cubism, so this was a natural course of study.

~ ~ ~

Tony straightened his tie, preparatory to visiting Peggy Sue. He had decided to initiate their conversation by discussing Picasso's *Girl With a Mandolin.* As he slapped on a touch of cologne, he tried not to fret at how he might disappoint her on their wedding night. Clench his eyes shut and conjure Lizzie Borden?

~ ~ ~

Simultaneously, Peggy Sue and Dave were in the shower at the Rosebud Motel, neither disappointed.

~ ~ ~

Brady asked the cab driver at the Quito airport to recommend a hotel and take him there. The driver's English wasn't the best, so Brady shouted at him until he understood.

Brady didn't know what he was going to do in Ecuador. He just knew he had to make an appearance, had to have proof he'd actually made the trip. Airline and hotel paperwork, a stamped passport, et cetera, to justify money spent. And to save his life.

He'd gotten drunk and gone to the airport the day following the call from the Neon Bitch and the transfer of the fifty grand. He'd gotten drunker at the airport and transferred airplanes at JFK (if memory served).

He sat at the Presidential Palace plaza getting his shoes shined by an urchin, gasping for oxygen at the 9350' altitude, wondering what next.

What to do?

23.

PHOSPHORUS. *Non-metallic and reactive, with the symbol P; Atomic number 15; Specific gravity of white phosphorus 1.823.*

Phosphorescence: an enduring luminescence without discernible heat.

Phosphorus is used in anti-personnel bombs, fertilizer, detergents, pesticides and matches.

Don Bruce Ripugnante sat in the dark, illuminating it in short intervals by igniting wooden matches, the kind with the phosphorus tip, listening to them sizzle in a bucket of water. He wore down one thumbnail and switched to the other.

This nonsensical activity kept his mind off of the plumbing rooter soon to spiral up his ass. It brought back fond memories too.

At age 16, he set his first arson fire. That was how he broke in with the neighborhood gang, setting fires to small businesses that didn't play ball. That one got out of control and raged through the apartments above the meat market, killing some old broad.

That wasn't his problem. It was just one of those things. She'd been at the wrong place at the wrong time was all. Bruce took over the gang at age 18 after burning down the home of the local boss, him inside too.

A knock on the door. He knew who it was and yelled to come in.

The man came in, trembling as he spoke. "Don Bruce, I have some news."

It was the guy assigned to trail his little girl.

"It ain't good or you wouldn't ask to come here."

The man didn't speak.

"What's she done now? This art bullshit of hers, is that part of it?"

"No sir. She's been with that reporter."

"The scumbag reporter out to get me?"

"Yes sir."

"What do you mean been with him?"

"*Been* with him."

"You gotta be kidding me."

"I wish I was."

Bruce Ripugnante yelled, "Where, when, what?"

The man flinched. "All night in a motel. More than once."

"No mistakes? *That* reporter?"

"Yes, Don Bruce."

"This JFK shit in his paper." Bruce's voice trailed off.

The man said nothing.

"This is for absolute sure, what you seen, Peggy Sue and him?"

"Yes, Don Bruce."

"Spitting in my face, she is. This little girl of mine, no respect. It's this freaky art she does and the weirdoes that do it that she knows, they got her head on sideways."

The man didn't answer.

"What we done to his car, it was a royal fuckup. The dummy you sent, he blew himself up, not what he was supposed to."

The man didn't answer.

"We need to get to the rat motherfucker's car. Pass the word on. Let Tony Whack know what you found out too. He hears about this, he'll be sure it's done right."

~ ~ ~

The listening device to her husband's master suite worked great. When they divided living quarters, he'd had it put in, to catch her if she was fooling around.

She'd had her suspicions and had her wing swept. The nerd who found the bugs made the system two-way and added an automatic recording device, like in Nixon's White House.

Madge Ripugnante sipped her mimosa, listening and thinking.

24.

PLATINUM. *Gorgeous, gray-white, and valuable with the symbol Pt; Atomic number 78; Specific gravity 21.4. Heavier than gold and almost as pricey, platinum is gold's rival in many ways.*

Tarnish-resistant, platinum is used in fine jewelry, automotive catalytic converters, and electrical contacts.

The man who visited Larry H. Olson in the state pen and took orders from him went to the newspaper reporter, but his primary topic was not water fluoridation.

"Platinum is nearly as spendy as gold," he told Dave Pomeroy. "It ain't chopped liver."

The biker sat in Dave's small cubicle. Dave wished he had a fan.

The biker wasn't partial to Dave either, a hard-ass little prick flipping a pencil in his hand, leaning back in his chair, a look on his face like he wanted to start something.

"I'm not a business reporter. I don't know the metals markets," he said. "So what?"

"What I mean is them platinum credit cards, where the sky's the, you know, the limit."

"I vaguely know of them."

"This guy we're with, he's locked up for having platinum."

Dave rocked forward. "For having a card he'd stolen?"

"For having about seventy-five platinum cards that didn't belong to him. That and other things they say he done."

Dave smiled. "That'd do it. That'd get you locked up."

"That watch you wrote about that was on the skeleton hand, the initials LHO belonged to Larry H. Olson, like that Lee Harry Oswald guy?"

"There's no end of coincidences."

"See, Larry took over the organization since Buford went and disappeared."

"Buford Frog Prince Poe?" Dave said.

"That's him. Larry had gave the watch to Buford or sold it to him or Buford liked it and just took it from him. One or the other. I don't know."

"You're assuming Frog Prince has gone to that big lily pad in the sky?"

The visitor just looked at him, the smart-mouth motherfucker.

Dave said, "Who do you think did Frog Prince?"

"Gotta be the Eye-talians, but go and prove it."

"What's the point of you coming here?" Dave said.

"I know who the other initials are."

"Great."

"If you can pull some strings in behalf of Larry, get him out before he dies of old age."

"No promises, but I can make a phone call or two," Dave lied. "Who's JLR?"

"It's this broad he used to shack with. Her name's Jane Richards. Full name, Jane Linda Richards. Jane L. Richards."

Dave wrote it down. "There has to be any number of Jane L. Richards in the world. What else do you have on her?"

"She gave the watch to Larry for his birthday."

"That helps very little."

"They broke up. I think she was a bartender, maybe still is. She's on the sauce big-time, drunk more than she ain't."

"I'll look into it."

"Oh yeah, one other thing. Can you check on how they flouridize the water in the pen? You know, drinking water."

"Flouridize?"

The biker scratched his swastika. "You know, that fluoride shit they put in the water."

"*Fluor*ine? *Fluor*idation?"

"That's it. Larry says they do it to keep the prisoners calm and behaving, like Hitler and them did."

"I will look into it," Dave lied again. "Definitely."

"Really?"

"You bet. Hey, I find out the truth, there might be a Pulitzer in it for me."

25.

RADIUM. *Powerful radioactive element with the symbol Ra; Atomic number 88: Specific gravity 5.0.*

Early in the 20th Century, radium was painted on watch dials by young women, so the numbers could be seen in the dark. The women licked their brushes to keep the tips pointed, with horrific damage to their health. The "radium girls" cases established the right of employees to sue employers for unsafe working conditions.

Radium is of no value whatsoever to living organisms.

Radium breaks down as radon gas, an alleged health problem in itself, wafting from the ground into dwellings. Thousands of lung cancer deaths have been blamed on it.

The doorbell wouldn't stop ringing, goddamnit.

She got up, head throbbing from her hangover.

She'd been drinking on the job again. A barkeep with a coffee cup on the counter with bourbon-rocks in it, that was a no-no. The manager gave her the boot and took over her shift.

With a sympathetic customer, she'd barhopped down the street, ending up with him here. Whoever he was, he was gone now. She hoped he hadn't stolen anything, like some of the bastards.

She threw on her bathrobe and answered the door to a guy carrying some sort of gizmo with a probe on it.

"Ma'am, sorry to bother you, but this is urgent."

"What's urgent?"

"I've been surveying the neighborhood and you have a serious radon problem."

"We do?"

"You do. Did you know that radon is the second leading cause of lung cancer deaths?"

"Gee."

"Yes ma'am. My firm can eliminate that for you and put your mind at ease. I can show you the data from my readings."

"Come on in, then. I have something to show you too. No, stay standing. This won't take a minute."

She went into her bedroom and got two things. She came out and said, "My great-grandmother was a radium girl. Do you remember hearing or reading of them?"

"I'm not sure."

"Well, way back when, they painted radium on wristwatch numbers so they'd show up in the dark. It was all the rage. They used fine fine brushes and licked the tips to keep them sharp. The poor girls developed terrible cancers. Here's picture of my great-grandma who I never met. My mother didn't get to know her either and my grandmother was real young when she died. Here's a picture of her."

The salesman made a face at the sight of a young woman with half of her lower jaw gone. "Gross."

"She lived maybe a month longer. She wasn't twenty-two years old."

"I'm sorry."

"No, you're not. Great-grandmother was part of the lawsuit that helped employees to sue if they have unsafe working conditions."

"Cool."

"So, you see, I'm very conscious of radium, how it breaks down as radon gas. I've never lived anyplace without being sure there's no radon."

"Actually, there are advanced tests in our system that *do* indicate radon here."

The lying bastard. A switch went off in Jane's marinated brain.

She took the second thing out of her pocket, a small pistol.

"What you're doing is lower than snakeshit. I'm gonna do one good thing for people once in my crummy life."

She shot him through the chest. He fell dead, landing upright in the sofa.

Jane sat down and began to light a cigarette. She put it back in the pack, wondering why the hell she did what she did.

She looked at the photo of her great granny, the young lady without all her lower jaw. The picture had given her many a nightmare, but for some reason she couldn't hide it away or throw it out.

Maybe what she just did she did for her.

She unzipped his pants and undid his belt.

Then she opened her robe, to take off her panties. Oops. No panties on. Her Romeo last night had probably taken them as a souvenir.

She went to the hamper for a dirty pair. She ripped them and slipped them on. She ripped her nightgown too.

Jane L. Richards ran outside screaming "rape" at the top of her lungs and waited for neighbors to call the police.

26.

SILVER. *A soft, white and lustrous metal with the symbol Ag: Atomic number 47; Specific gravity 10.49.*

Used in chemical catalysts, pricey tableware; ornaments, jewelry, mirrors, and electrical contacts.

Antonio (Tony Whack Job) Spazento was livid. He was heartbroken too.

He'd just gotten the news. His intended was a no-good slattern.

But to fornicate with that reporter? Why, she was disrespecting everyone close to her. Tony wasn't opposed to her banging somebody on the side after their sacred vows; it'd take the heat off him to perform, Lizzie Borden or no Lizzie Borden. But *anybody* in the world except that reporter!

He'd personally supervise modifications to Pomeroy's land yacht. He'd be absolutely certain it was done right.

If that didn't kill him and merely send him to the hospital, he'd see him there, bring flowers and a small pistol.

He'd dispatch him with a silver bullet. The man deserved to die as if a werewolf. He'd add some humor to what had to be done.

He'd attend his funeral.

He'd urinate in his coffin.

The night after the funeral, he'd dig him up.

He'd urinate on him again.

He'd take him away and chop him up into the tiniest pieces.

27.

SODIUM. *A silvery alkali metal with the symbol Na; Atomic number 11; Specific gravity 0.968. If you toss the pure metal into water, stand back; it'll be the 4th of July.*

Sodium chloride (NaCl) is table salt, the most common use of sodium. It is an essential element for humans if not consumed in quantity; 2300 mg. per days is the recommended maximum.

Used too in lye and sodium vapor lights.

Jane L. Richards thrust off hands of the concerned and ran back inside seconds before the police and ambulance arrived. She stepped around the corpse and sprinkled a dash of table salt in her eyes. It hurt like hell, but produced tears and reddened her eyes.

She staggered back outside, screaming and sniffling, eyes running, an increasingly authentic victim of attempted rape.

~ ~ ~

Meanwhile, No-Neck's normal voice was returning. Kind of. He sounded like a Latvian tourist, although he'd never been east of Brooklyn.

"We oughta slip lye in his coffee. Turn his throat into a blast furnace. Can we do that?"

"He drinks it black," Tony Whack Job told the cretin.

They were in the self-storage unit rented by Dave Pomeroy. On a dolly, with a trouble light, their prison-trained mechanic, their "iron" expert, was underneath the reporter's land yacht.

He rolled out and said, "His next ride's his last."

Tony Whack Job closed his eyes, visions of Picasso's *Girl With a Mandolin* dancing like sugarplums.

~ ~ ~

Brady awakened to slurping. He was in a field and his head rested against a salt lick he shared with a steer. There was a volcano in the distance and his pockets were turned inside out.

Everything was gone. Money, wallet, passport, everything.

He was cruelly hungover, yesterday a total blank. He'll have to hitchhike back into Quito, clean up in his room if he still had a room, and request political asylum.

What else can he do?

~~ ~

Iggy had bad vibes. Transmissions from the Martians were so staticky that he couldn't make out one word in ten. The remains of lunch had lodged between his teeth, shorting out his fillings. Upstairs and outside, enemy agents were hacking his teeth too, collecting vital data. He knew it.

The items he'd ordered from his security director came just fine: triple cheeseburgers, porn magazines, sodium bicarbonate, razor blades, and sodium vapor lamps to beam onto the lead like the Martians had advised.

But there were extras he'd found, which must have been planted while he slept, doped up by the security team. There had been a metallic taste in yesterday's French fries too.

No less than three bugs: one inside a light switch cover, one under his workbench stool, one taped to the underside of the toilet lid.

They overhear and oversee all.

On a secure (so far) laptop, he placed a large order to Communist Red China.

~ ~ ~

Bruce Ripugnante Junior's Vegas apartment had been trashed, turned inside out, and his Escalade was gone from its parking space. They'd missed his emergency stash, a roll of hundreds taped to the back of the garbage disposal motor.

Junior hopped an *el cheapo* flight, bound for the only person who understood him.

28.

SULFUR. *Soft, yellow and smelly with the symbol S; Atomic number 16; Specific gravity 1.96.*

Sulfur (also spelled sulphur) is known in the Bible as brimstone.

Sulfur is used in fertilizer, sulfuric acid and winemaking.

The phony radon salesman was a parishioner of a fire-and-brimstone church. This church made the wildest holy rollers and snake handlers seem moderate, intelligent and enlightened.

The church's pastor said no words at the radon man's funeral because he had had no funeral yet. The departed remained in the cooler at the medical examiner's office, pending completion of the investigation of his shooting.

When the stiff was released for burial, the pastor would find excuses to be elsewhere. The rapist wannabe wouldn't be acknowledged on Sunday either.

In his mind, even though this woman was probably asking for it, rapists were scarcely one step above sodomites, Arabs, coloreds, Jews and Democrats.

~ ~ ~

When Del wasn't out drinking beer as he drove around and played with his metal detector, he dabbled in winemaking. The results were putrid.

He blamed the foul bouquet and fouler taste on spoilage. Age did not bring forth hints of blackberry or cassis or apricot or nutmeg or any of that other shit in the snooty-snoot wine magazines.

Del abandoned the organic approach and added sulfur dioxide (SO2). If the commercial vintners did it to control fermentation and stabilize their product, why the hell not?

He gave it a reasonable time to age (the following Thursday).

He uncapped a bottle, experienced a hint of sulfur dioxide, and pronounced it drinkable.

~ ~ ~

Bruce Ripugnante Junior's plane landed. He rented a car, bought a cell phone, drove to a bar, and waited until dark.

He went out to the car and made a call.

"I'm in town and really need help."

The woman recognized his voice.

She said, "You've been a naughty boy."

Junior didn't reply.

"What do you want?"

"I'm damn near tapped out and I need somewhere to go until I figure things out and get back on my feet."

"Do you have a car?"

"Yeah."

"Leave it on the street a block or two away and be at the side gate in an hour."

"Yes, Mommy."

29.

THALLIUM. *A soft gray metal with the symbol Ti; Atomic number 81; Specific gravity 11.85.*

Used in optics and electronics.

A chic poison in the 1950s, thallium was known as "the poisoner's poison" or "inheritance powder", as arsenic had been. It was a "foolproof" murder weapon, like dropping a frozen Thanksgiving turkey on somebody from the third-floor landing, then cooking it.

Don Bruce Ripugnante's consigliore was an odd little guy. Pinstripes that had to cost in the four figures. Wide rimless glasses. Hair combed from where it grew to where it didn't. The rock in his pinkie ring had to be six carats.

"He still down there in that Mexican country?"

"Yes, Don Bruce. Ecuador."

"He playing games with our money like you said?"

The consigliore nodded. "No surprises. Going outside the family for this was my mistake, a failed experiment. I wished to render transparency opaque, to establish a firewall. It won't happen again."

"Whatever you said, how much dough are we out?"

"Less than ten grand. We have reacquired the rest."

"It ain't sinking in how we were gonna make out on this."

"Well, we keep the IRS out of our business by a combination of shell corporations and the tax codes of this country, Ecuador, and also the Grand Cayman —"

Don Bruce Ripugnante lifted a hand. "Okay, whatever you say. You're the expert on this. What about that rat motherfucker who hustled us?"

"He was taken for a ride. He has no option but to go to his hotel room. He has no ID, no money. He must subsist on food and drink there at their cafe, on credit, which an Ecuadorian in our employ is adulterating with thallium. It was once known as the poisoner's poison or inheritance powder. The local authorities may or may not be able to determine whether or not he died of natural causes. If they even care to."

"Ain't no reason somebody else besides me shouldn't have a tummy ache."

To be continued in **34. ZIRCONIUM.**

~ ~ ~

Madge Ripugnante and her son, Bruce Ripugnante Junior, sat, drinking mimosas, listening to her husband and his father, chatting with his consigliore.

30.

TIN. *Soft, silvery shiny, easy to melt, with the symbol Sn; Atomic number 50; Specific gravity 7.3.*

The first manmade alloy, in use since 3000 BC, was bronze, a mix of copper and tin.

Pewter, mostly tin, was the common flatware until 100 years ago.

Used these days for solder and in metal plating. Sheet steel is known in the auto body and scrap yard trades as "tin".

DAVE POMEROY: That is a tragic story about your great-grandmother.

JANE L. RICHARDS: Thank you so much for listening, Mr. Pomeroy. I needed to vent and I need the public to know the full truth.

DAVE: But the photo of her had nothing to do with you protecting yourself in the rape attempt? I'm confused.

JANE: No, it didn't. I think when he showed him the picture, it turned him on. A real sicko. He was all over me, his hands —

DAVE: Know what I think, Jane?

JANE: No.

DAVE: That you're full of shit. I don't know why you killed him, but it wasn't attempted rape.

JANE: Fuck you. You weren't there.

DAVE: Talk to me about Larry H. Olson.

JANE: Who?"

DAVE: Jane.

JANE: I knew him. So what?

DAVE: You knew him well enough to give him a watch inscribed 'From JLR to LHO'.

JANE: It was a cheap watch, made in China out of tin and plastic. The inscription cost me more than the watch. He was a cheap bastard, so it's all he deserved.

DAVE: Its last stop was a severed hand that was buried in a field. It behooves you to remember.

JANE: Is that a threat?

DAVE: Yes it is.

JANE: What do you want?

DAVE: Does the name Buford Poe mean anything to you?

JANE: Frog Prince. I saw him maybe twice. Him and Larry hung out. Poe was super creepy. Ever seen him?

DAVE: He's missing in action. Am I taking a wild stab in the dark by saying it was his hand the watch was attached to?

JANE: Stabs in the dark is what you do. I read your trashy paper. How the hell should I know? Larry gave it to him? Sold it to him? Ask Larry.

DAVE: I'll write the story the way you'd like, one woman's gallant defense against a violent sex fiend. The feminist police will erect a statue of you.

JANE: Is that a bribe?

DAVE: Yes it is.

JANE: Okay, Poe was a blowhard. He'd have a few and talk how tough he was, how him and his bikers muscled in on other people's action. He could've taken the watch. He'd steal anything that wasn't nailed down.

DAVE: The last time you saw him, who was he muscling in on?

JANE: Some junkyard. Chuck's, I think it was. He was going to set up a chop shop there.

DAVE: All right, let's get back to where you tore away from the psycho rapist as he was tearing at your unmentionables.

JANE: Are you married or going with anyone? We could do the interview in person, you know.

DAVE: I have a call waiting.

~ ~ ~

Dave would have told her that even if he hadn't a call waiting.

But he did.

It was Madeleine.

31.

TITANIUM. *Lustrous and silvery, very strong for its weight, with the symbol Ti; Atomic number 22; Specific gravity 4.507.*

Used as an alloy in industrial, aerospace and recreational hardware.

It's very important in airliners, in components such as landing gear and wing struts, where high strength and low weight is critical.

Blended titanium alloys utilized in aircraft can cost $150 per pound; pure titanium found in golf clubs goes for about $7 a pound.

After returning Madeleine's call, Dave Pomeroy started his land yacht and let it warm up and contaminate the atmosphere with non-emission-controlled exhaust.

Thinking.

He drove out, bound for Chuck's Waste Management and Recycling. His 1957 DeSoto Adventurer ragtop with gold accents was to be a conversation piece there, an icebreaker.

The storage facility was atop a shallow hill, the next stop a busy intersection controlled by a traffic light.

As Dave approached it, he stepped on the brake. The pedal was spongy. Then it hit to the floor.

He pumped and pumped and tried to downshift, pushing buttons on the push-button tranny. They were useless, as if disconnected.

The gas pedal plunged to the floor.

He hoped like hell for a green light.

Or even an amber.

He got red.

Dave laid on the horn.

Out of order too.

Two-plus-tons of Detroit iron accelerated through Sixth and Hoover.

Dave cranked hard to the left; the power steering was malfunctioning.

The DeSoto went up on two wheels. Dave hung on.

Motor vehicles of that era had no seat belts. Keeping with authenticity, he hadn't installed them.

On Sixth, headed for Jackson, on a steeper hill, he slalomed, creasing a parked car on his right, veering him into the left lane.

To avoid a head-on, a car went up the sidewalk, smashing into a discount furniture storefront.

Sixth and Jackson was a six-way intersection, joining Market Street on the diagonal.

What are the odds of getting a green light?

One in three or four.

He got a yellow arrow that became a red arrow that became solid red.

Dave was nailed simultaneously from each direction: a small (relatively) SUV to his right front, a midsize sedan to his left rear, a medium-sized (relatively) SUV to his right, shearing off the tailfin, a small hatchback that was almost through.

The hatchback's liftgate popped open. Objects flew out and smashed against the DeSoto's windshield, spidering it.

Dave was spun 180-degrees and ended up half on the street. He slammed against the steering wheel and caromed into the passenger door.

The objects that had flown onto his hood were titanium golf clubs, broken and bent now.

Bruised and bleeding, Dave crawled through the driver's window.

The golf-club owner was screaming at him, saying he'd bought them on sale not an hour ago and calling him a drunk and a piece of shit.

Dave ignored him, leaned against a wall, and called Josh.

Josh listened, then yelled into the city room, "Stop the presses!"

Meanwhile, police and aid vehicles arrived at the scene. Thankfully, nobody was hurt beyond bumps and bruises, Dave by far the worst. He declined a ride in an ambulance. Dave didn't know how many air bags deployed altogether in the combined vehicles, but they sure did their job.

Josh arrived in the Taurus with a beat reporter and a photographer.

"How do you feel?" Josh asked him.

"Worse than I ever have after a football game, but we're gonna sell some papers," he said, limping to and past Josh. "I'm commandeering the Taurus."

Josh got in with him, saying, "Wherever you think you're going, I'm riding shotgun."

They went to Chuck's Waste Management and Recycling Dave had a wallet photo of the DeSoto, a pin-up, thinking he could bond with it.

But hell no.

Not after this.

No preamble of any kind.

The newspapermen walked into Chuck's shack/office. Dave showed ID and said, "Chuck-o, your Mob bosses sabotaged my car."

Seated at a filthy, cluttered desk, Chuck shook his head, jowls trailing. "I don't know what you're talking about. I'm self-employed. I got no bosses."

With his left index finger, his right arm being too sore to lift, Dave pointed to the hill directly east of downtown and the old homes that comprised the city's first residential area.

"See up there, Chuck? We have paid informants on a line of sight with you. Know what they've seen?"

Chuck shook his head.

"We've equipped them with infra-red goggles, the kind where things look green during the night."

"Those babies cost a bundle," Josh said. "Wiped out our budget for the year."

Chuck looked at Josh and then Dave.

"Ten minutes before my accidentally-on-purpose accident, one of my top informants called. She watches your junkyard day and night. She sees suspicious activity, and she's seen a bunch, which she snaps pictures with a top-of-the-line super-zoom camera."

In fact, Madeleine had called Dave to say in frustration that she had not seen anything whatsoever incriminating.

Dave had intended to gently bluff Chuck, hoping for a slip up. That was before he was transformed into a walking, talking, bleeding bruise.

"We have hard evidence that you are the proud owner of Frog Prince Poe's body. Be sure to read tomorrow's headline. It'll be the same size type as Pearl Harbor was."

Chuck scratched inside his coveralls.

"The hand and forearm bone in the field ought to be a perfect match."

Chuck opened his mouth, then closed it.

"The Ripugnantes will drop you like a two-bit whore. You're it, pal."

Josh handed him a flask from a jacket pocket. "It's good for what ails you."

Chuck took a long pull, wiped his mouth with the back of his hand, and said, "You got one of them witness protection deals you can set me up with?"

Josh went outside and made some calls. When the state police and FBI arrived, he called the news team at the "accident" scene and told them to get on over. Hitchhike if they had to.

"I made some witness-protection arrangements for you. Chuck," Josh lied.

"I need to get back and start my story," Dave said.

He tried to get up, but collapsed like a pile of laundry.

"Journalism is out of your hands for the moment, my friend," Josh said, dialing nine-one-one.

*****

Peggy Sue Ripugnante was doing an abstract expressionist work of Tom & Geri's Rosebud Motel. With titanium white, applied thickly, outlining the exterior shape in fast-drying acrylic, smoothing the L-shaped building's edges and sections to the phallic.

Madge Ripugnante sat with her, drinking coffee, looking semi-matronly in a clean bathrobe. She had gone from her wing of Tara to her daughter's suite, unseen by her estranged husband, who continued to sit in the dark, feeling sorry for himself.

"What next?" Madge said.

"It'll be mixed media. Gouache. Tempera. A collage. I'm not sure."

"Phallic symbols?"

"Mother," she said, laughing.

"You must persuade your father to go in for the colonoscopy. If he dies, there will be a war for succession. Spazento, your fiancé, will be a big player."

"He's *not* my fiancé. And how do you know all this?"

117

"I know many things."

Peggy Sue's phone rang.

"Hello."

"Yes."

"How did you get this number?"

"They did what to him?"

"He's where?"

"Oh my god! I'll be right there."

She flipped the phone shut and said, "Dave's in the hospital."

"Go, Dear. Go."

On the way out, Peggy Sue almost ran into her father, who was coming from the kitchen with s TV dinner.

"Hey, where's the fire?"

"Your goons tampered with Dave Pomeroy's car. I'm going to see him at the hospital."

"You can't do that. I'm telling you. Stay away from him. I'm ordering you."

"You go in to the clinic like you should, I'll be there for you too," Peggy Sue said, running by him. "Otherwise, go straight to hell!"

32.

TUNGSTEN. *A heavy and versatile metal with the symbol W: Atomic number 74; Specific gravity 19.3.*

The "W" stands for wolfram or wolframite, which is tungsten ore.

The metal is used in tungsten carbide, other alloys, catalysts, and light bulb filaments.

Tungsten has the highest melting point of any metal.

Tungsten is 1.7 times as heavy as lead and exactly as heavy as gold.

Iggy had the package of lead billets he'd ordered overnighted from Communist Red China.

The Chinks charged a fortune to do it, but when you were batshit crazy and had $331 million at your disposal, damn the cost.

Lead billets from halfway around the world. Nutty as a fruitcake, the security director thought yet again. That was why he let them pass through unopened, uninspected and unreported to the Ripugnantes.

Five hand truckloads of lead billets that cost a fortune to ship were wheeled through the side door into Iggy's basement digs.

Iggy waited until the dark of night until all was quiet upstairs, then peeled open the boxes.

There were no lead billets inside the boxes marked as lead billets. They were gold ingots, or so the gold-plated tungsten looked and felt like.

This was how Iggy converted lead into gold. It's the way the Martians said to do it. The Chinamen grew most of the world's tungsten. They sold it pure, in alloys and gold-plated. The customer was always right.

Then Iggy flushed the three bugs they'd planted down the toilet. They could chase him through the sewer system, fighting off the alligators.

Iggy shredded the Red China paperwork, which included extra charges for labeling the boxes of gold-plated tungsten "lead billets". He spread the billets out all over the place, and went out the basement door to join Mommy in Biarritz before she married one of those slick young guys who were sticking their weenies in her.

He'd leave his pseudo-fortune for the boys upstairs.

Let them kill each other over it.

Like the Martians said they would.

~ ~ ~

The security man on night-watch duty had dozed off. He awakened to funny noises from all three bugs. Like water running hard and bubbling, like the nut case downstairs was river rafting.

He woke up the crew chief, who woke everybody else up.

They went downstairs to find the retard gone and bars of gold all over the place.

They picked some up, hefting them.

"Heavy," one said.

"What the deal is," the crew chief said. "He couldn't alchemate lead into gold, so he went and bought it."

"How come he split, leaving the gold?"

The crew chief tapped his temple. "He ain't right up there."

"Maybe he went to get a truck."

Nobody spoke for a moment.

"We gotta tell the Don right away."

"I tried. Couldn't reach him. I dunno why."

"Since that newspaper guy got a hard-on for him, he been keeping what you call a low profile."

After a moment of silence and exchanged glances, the crew chief said, "We do all the work and take all the chances, and the bosses spoon the cream off the top. I say we divvy up on our own. Anyone got a problem with that?"

No one spoke.

"Okay, let's get to work. I got places to go, things to see."

They carried off what they could carry and went their separate ways, destined for disappointment.

And much worse, just as the Martians had said.

~ ~ ~

With Chuck's direction, Poe's body wasn't difficult to find.

Chuck said, "When do I get to go, do you know where you'll be stashing me?"

An FBI agent said, "In due time. After you give us a sworn statement."

"Okay. Let's not take all day."

~ ~ ~

Peggy Sue sat at Dave's bedside. He was wrapped, bandaged and stitched.

He awoke, groggy.

She kissed his forehead and told him that she loved him.

He said he loved her, patted the bed, and said that there was all kinds of room.

She got in with him and gently snuggled.

"Let me kiss you where it hurts and make you well," she whispered.

~ ~ ~

At sunrise, Bruce Ripugnante Senior drove to the clinic.

His phone had been off, so he was missing all the excitement.

The shit was hitting the fan and he would not appreciate the pun.

If the only way to keep his little girl's love was to have a drain cleaner rammed up his dirt chute, so be it.

~ ~ ~

"You have two choices, Junior," Madge said.

"What are they?"

"To see your father at the clinic now or see your father at the clinic later."

"I don't get it. And I don't want to."

"Don't whine. If you refuse, you're out of this house for good."

"Hey, c'mon."

"The earlier you see him, the groggier he'll be from the medication and a lesser chance he'll fly into an uncontrollable rage."

"I get it. I'm on my way, Mommy."

33.

XENON. *A colorless, odorless and heavy gas, with the symbol Xe; Atomic number 54; Specific gravity .0059.*

Xenon is a noble gas, meaning that it is very stable and has a low reaction rate.

Xenon is used in optics, lasers and anesthetics.

It has been controversial of late because it's the key ingredient in HID (high-intensity-discharge) headlamps. If aimed incorrectly they are blinding to oncoming traffic.

In Chuck's statement to the interviewing officers as Buford Poe's remains were located and bagged, "Tony Whack Job, he said it was an accident."

"You believe in the tooth fairy, Chuck?"

"Hey, if Tony Whack's looking you in the eyeball and says it's an accident, it's an accident."

~ ~ ~

That very evening, Antonio Spazento entered the hospital and Dave Pomeroy's room, carrying a bouquet of flowers. A curtain was drawn around the bed. He tossed the flowers aside and oh so carefully opened the curtain.

Naked but for bandages and dressing was his quarry. His eyes were closed. Easy pickings.

Tony wanted Pomeroy to see who was sending him to his maker. If there was no autopsy, the reporter's demise would be attributed to a cerebral hemorrhage.

He leaned close and whispered, "Time to rise and shine, sleepyhead."

Groggy from pain medication, Dave smelled Peggy Sue's perfume. But it was different, sort of like men's cologne. He knew he was fuzzyheaded, and what did it matter anyway? He reached for her, mumbling, "Hop on in. I saved your spot."

Dave's muscular hand rubbed Tony's buttocks and thigh, arousing him.

Unthinking, obeying primal instincts, picturing Lizzie Border in that bed, Tony dropped his baby pistol, unzipped, and unfastened his belt.

Peggy Sue came into the room after a trip to the bathroom. She was wearing only a hospital gown, which she began to remove.

She saw the man who was her designated fiancé climbing into bed with the man she wanted more than anything in the whole, wide world to be her fiancé.

"Oh my God!"

Pants wadded at his ankles, Tony and his erection turned, facing her and her nakedness. It was a toss-up who was more repelled.

"It's not what you think," he said nonsensically.

"I had a hunch about you. On our dates, you didn't try a thing."

"I was showing respect."

"You lectured me on wine when you should have been playing footsy."

Tony pulled up his pants and stepped toward her. He'd do them both, side by side. A pair of cerebral hemorrhages.

"You sicko, you were going to take advantage of him!"

"No. Please," he said, reaching down for his .25 automatic. "I can explain."

"Rape!" Peggy Sue screamed. "Rape!"

His world topsy-turvy, Tony had an epiphany. He'd catch the next flight to the Cayman Islands, where he'd visit his money.

Out a side door and down the corridor he went, into the parking lot, and into his car.

On a two-lane highway, the last stretch to the airport, Tony could see the runways. Ten more minutes and he'd be in parking garage. Fun and sun and who knows what awaited. Husky, surly native girls like in the South Seas?

A jacked-up, custom-exhaust, blackout-window, Xenon-headlamp kiddy car was coming in the opposite direction. The 19-year-old driver had been smoking a little weed, but was alert enough to see a dead opossum on the road just ahead. Or at least he thought he did.

His car was lowered within an inch of the ground and had a princess-and-the-pea ride. Hitting the critter would do some serious damage, so he swerved around it.

He was in no danger of hitting the oncoming vehicle, but his Xenon headlamps temporarily blinded the driver.

Antonio (Tony Whack Job) Spazento was not a man to use foul language, but made an exception as he swerved onto the shoulder. His tires caught on gravel, spinning him back onto the road and across the centerline, where his Cadillac was met by the vehicle behind the kiddy car. It was an 18-wheeler whose driver was texting his girlfriend in Turpentine Springs, Texas.

*****

The state police and FBI burst into the clinic ex-employee/head clerk Judith knew as the DCOR (Discretion Clinic for the Obscenely Rich). They had an arrest warrant for Bruce Ripugnante and found him in stirrups, proctologist and assistants at the ready.

"Holy shit!" said a technician holding a tray of tools.

"You got that right," an agent said.

Barely able to contain his laughter, another agent bent over, turned his head, and read Tony his rights.

Bruce Junior had been in the waiting room where he'd have to face the old man after the surgery. He hadn't liked the look of all those cops rushing in.

He's been looking at the pictures in a car magazine. He tossed it aside and scrammed.

Mommy would understand.

Wouldn't she?

34.

ZIRCONIUM. *A lustrous grey-white metal with the symbol Zr: Atomic number 40; Specific gravity 6.52.*

Zirconium has many obscure industrial applications and one that isn't.

Zirconium dioxide (ZrO2), of which one form is cubic zirconia.

Bruce Ripugnante's colostomy test was negative, harmless polyps removed.

~ ~ ~

The grand jury's decision was likewise negative. Ripugnante was indicted on 157 charges, going back to a fatal arson fire he'd set at age 16.They had been filed largely based on the content of recorded conversations that had been anonymously mailed to them over a period of time.

Chuck's sworn statement was the clincher.

~ ~ ~

Peggy Sue's and Dave's wedding, Crusading Reporter and Mafia Princess, if not the city's wedding of the year, was the most fascinating. It was being held in the city's largest art gallery, where a one-person show was being held for the abstraction expressionist works of the bride-to-be. Filling the entire back wall was a Jackson Pollock-esque oil on plywood. A red dot on the identifying placard indicated that it had been sold.

The father of the bride was unavailable to give her away, despite protestations that he wasn't a flight risk, which he was. His place was taken by a nattily-dressed gentleman who wore rimless glasses and combed his hair from where it grew to where it didn't. Peggy Sue knew the shadowy individual as Uncle Niccolo.

Having been invited, Madeleine wanted to doll up. She bought a dress and went to a jeweler to shop for a bracelet that matched the ring Lan had given her. Out of curiosity, she had the ring appraised.

"It's a nice cubic zirconia. The yellowish tint is due to a trace of nitrogen," the jeweler said. "It's easily worth sixty or seventy bucks."

"Oh."

"That's with the setting."

"Oh."

Madeleine went home, got online, and began shopping for thallium.

See **29. THALLIUM.**

Thank you for reading.

Please review this book. Reviews help others find Absolutely Amazing eBooks and inspire us to keep providing these marvelous tales.

If you would like to be put on our email list to receive updates on new releases, contests, and promotions, please go to AbsolutelyAmazingEbooks.com and sign up.

About the Author

A prolific author, Gary Alexander has written a dozen and a half novels and more than 150 short stories. One story appeared in *Best American Mystery Stories 2010*, another in *Ice Cold*, last year's Mystery Writers of America anthology. Alexander is a nonsmoking, nondrinking vegetarian. He does, however, abuse caffeine and chocolate.

The New
Atlantian Library

New AtlantianLibrary.com
or AbsolutelyAmazingEbooks.com
or AA-eBooks.com

www.ingramcontent.com/pod-product-compliance
Lightning Source LLC
Chambersburg PA
CBHW050410030726
47503CB00006B/2127